CRUSADER

SAINT TOMMY, NYPD BOOK FIVE

DECLAN FINN

SILVER EMPIRE

Dedicated to Poland.
An island of light on a continent falling into darkness.

PROLOGUE: LAST TOUR BUS TO MUNICH

Adara was hiding from the monsters.

She had been in the bathroom when the bus stopped. She had been afraid to come out when the growling started. The roars. The screams.

She would have stayed in the bathroom, but that seemed too simple. There was nowhere to hide if someone thought about it. She was small, but she wasn't small enough to hide behind the toilet.

When all of the others had been taken off the bus, she slid out of the bathroom on her belly and crawled on her elbows all the way to the back row. She grabbed the back chair and pulled herself under it. She was still small for her age, and so she could fit where the carry-on luggage used to go.

It was just her and her wine-dark shirt and her long black skirt. The only thing she heard for the longest time was the sound of her own breathing. She forced herself to quiet even that as she curled her legs up against her and held tight.

Clomp.

Someone had stepped back onto the bus.

Adara stopped breathing entirely and closed her eyes tight.

Click. Thump. Click Thump.

The footsteps came slow and careful, coming steadily closer.

Adara forced herself to breathe out slowly, so she didn't gasp.

Click thump ... pause.

Adara froze mid-breath. She had barely inhaled when the footsteps stopped.

Click-thump. Click-thump.

She felt the footsteps through the bus floor.

Click-thump. Click-thump.

It was so close now. It was right behind her.

Click-thump. Stop.

She could feel it above her, through the seats. She heard it breathing.

Then the other breathing stopped.

Adara slowly, carefully, let out her own breath.

A hand grabbed her ankles and dragged her away as she screamed.

1 / UNTO US A CHILD IS BORN

Chattanooga, Tennessee

I WOKE UP TO MY WIFE SCREAMING.

"Tommy! Wake up!"

I sat up in bed like Count Orlac from the silent film *Nosferatu*. I didn't quite shoot straight up and out of a coffin, but it was close. I grabbed the gun from my nightstand and snapped around to face her, gun at the ready.

Nothing ominous or threatening was in the room. I grabbed her hand. "What is it? What's the matter?"

Mariel looked at me with a loving gaze that also said *Stop being stupid.* "My water broke."

Despite the natural inclinations of many civilians I had seen in similar situations, this news caused me to relax. It wasn't a demon. It wasn't zombies. It wasn't a SWAT team kicking in the door. This made for a nice change.

I checked the time. It was three in the morning. "Okay. Time to make the doughnuts."

I turned on the light and started getting dressed.

Our son Jeremy darted into the room, launching himself from the bedroom door to the bed. "Is she coming?"

Mariel smiled a little. "Yes, dear. We're going to have to go."

Jeremy nodded and shot off again to get dressed. Mariel watched me intently for a long moment but made no move to get off the bed—which was fine with me. I was going to help her out of bed once I was ready.

It took me a moment to realize that Mariel wasn't watching me as much as she was examining my scars.

Ever since my battle with the shadows in London, the scars had been solidifying, and I had to stretch them out. Anyone who looked closely at my body would easily confuse the new scars for stigmata. They were the size of quarters in the palms and the back of my hands, the soles and tops of my feet, and what looked like a through-and-through with a spear in my side.

Frankly, "stigmata" would be easier to explain to people than *"This is how I died once when I was bi-locating during riots in London and got eaten alive by shadows."*

"You realize that this isn't the worst thing that happened to me," I said, showing her my palm.

Mariel was about to speak, then had to stop and take several slow, deep breaths. "I wasn't exactly happy with your Saint Sebastian scars either."

I winced at the memory of those scars. A demon had ripped out a series of prison bars and proceeded to pin me to a concrete wall like a butterfly. I had died that time too.

Saint Paul said it was up to man only once to die ... boy, he didn't count on me. Then again, he also said, "I die daily," so he was still up on me by a few. I'm not that bad yet.

"Hey," I said aloud. "I'm still kicking."

The three of us ended up in the car that WitSec had provided. Chattanooga was a nice little town by our standards. It felt very much like our back end of Queens. Even "downtown" felt very much like our home. If we never went back to New York City, I wouldn't have been put off. Thankfully, anything not covered by the Witness Protection Program and the Marshal Service was covered by my NYPD salary—which I still collected while I was abroad. I was still on the active payroll since the NYPD is the only city police force I knew of that had foreign operatives. Money went a lot farther in Chattanooga than in Queens.

I wasn't terribly worried about my home in Queens. Given that my home was within three blocks of the precinct, it had become a makeshift crash pad for guys pulling double shifts. My partner, Alex Packard, had moved in permanently to maintain the place. He didn't have to worry about his apartment, as he sublet it to some college students.

Since there were still small platoons of assassins who still thought there was a bounty on my head, Packard had padded his arrest record with the idiots who thought I still lived there. *Nice when you do not have to chase them because they come to you.*

As I drove, I kept my speed level and easy. Breaking speed limits would only make it worse. But thankfully, I wasn't in a part of the world that really paid much attention to the posted speed limits. We made it to the hospital within twenty minutes. Mariel was in a bed five minutes after that.

Jeremy and I stayed with Mariel for the first hour. He and I alternated coaching her through her breathing. Since Mariel had been homeschooling Jeremy during the entire WitSec ordeal, Jeremy had been to as many Lamaze classes as I had. He was eager to help. Every time he took over, I alternated with praying the rosary.

Halfway through the second hour, doctors had taken notice of my hands – too many for Mariel's comfort. She gripped my hand and said, "Tommy, take Jeremy for a walk, would you?"

I just smiled, returned the quick squeeze, and went out into the hallway.

Jeremy looked around before saying at a whisper, "Dad, what happened to your hand that Mom's worried about it?"

I smiled at him. Jeremy had always thought of my charisms as superpowers ... which was the easiest way to understand them, really. He wanted to keep my powers a secret identity. To him, I was the next best thing to having Captain America for a father.

"I did a six-way split in London. One of me didn't end well."

He nodded solemnly. I didn't tell Jeremy that I had died five times in London during the riot. Calling my bisection "creating doubles" was misleading. I was in several places at once. It was one consciousness directing six bodies. I felt everything that had happened to each body. Thankfully, I had only kept a specific set of scars from one of the five deaths. It would have been difficult to explain dinosaur-like teeth marks traveling up my body.

"With great power comes great responsibility," he intoned. "Also, a lot of bruising. But why is Mom worried?"

"She's concerned that doctors are going to ask too many questions."

Jeremy frowned. He was probably trying to fit it to a classic superhero plot.

I had no doubt that he would find it, but I wanted a chair and a place for the two of us to sit back and relax.

We sat. Within five minutes, Jeremy was asleep, curled up against my side. I had one arm around Jeremy, the other hand fingering my rosary.

I fell asleep a little bit later. Chattanooga was one of the few places I felt comfortable enough to do that. It helped that every other citizen was armed. It wasn't Switzerland but close enough for me.

Around 8, a nurse prodded us awake.

After five hours of labor, Grace Gabrielle Nolan was born, weighing in at 8 pounds, 2 ounces. And she was adorable. I held her in one arm and held my wife's hand in the other. Mariel was still exhausted from the labor ... or was it because the labor started when she only had three hours of sleep? Either way, she was out like a light a few minutes after delivery. This left Jeremy and me to fill out the paperwork.

Jeremy and I planned for a day full of religious education since he had fallen into the faith as a way of researching my "superpowers." Though I was content to listen. I had been too busy getting shot at to investigate what "powers" I *might* possibly receive at some point, including Saints who raised the dead.

I had been listening to Jeremy so intently that I was only distracted when the loud *thump* of the cane was already upon us.

2 / WITNESS FOR THE PROSECUTION

I turned around to see a big man, over six feet tall, with a puffy, snowy white beard. The width of his gut exceeded his shoulder span, but not by much. For his age, he looked good. He was dressed in full, three-piece pinstripe suit. His tie was green and gold, something regimental, and vaguely Irish. His walking stick was a little taller. He was leaning heavily on it. Though it looked like an iron club. It was very sturdy but obviously an open-carry weapon.

"Jeremy, do you remember Assistant District Attorney William Carlton?" I asked my son.

He nodded enthusiastically, as though his favorite uncle had arrived. "Sure! Hey!"

Carlton thumped his way down the hall a little more and nodded in our direction. "Hello, Jeremy. Detective."

I forcibly kept my smile on my face. On one hand, I was certain that he was here to ask for a favor, and that favor had to be back in New York. I didn't begrudge him the favor he was certain to ask. I technically owed him. He was instrumental in the current deal that had me overseas for several months. While my friend

Father Freeman and the Mysterious Fed had proposed it to the acting mayor, ADA Carlton had gone to bat for me.

However, we were friendly but not friends. He couldn't have heard about Grace's birth. I hadn't even told my partner back in New York yet, and he was close enough to qualify as family. Thus, Carlton needed a favor. No one would go that far to ask after one's health. He wouldn't need me for my detective skills. After all, he had legions back home.

What he needed from me was my special relationship with God—though I couldn't imagine what.

Though I wasn't eager to go. I had spent the last month almost nonstop with my family as I awaited the Vatican's next recall order. It was Heaven. Morning Mass, followed by breakfast with the family, followed by Jeremy's education—at the current rate of speed, he'd be done with high school before he was fifteen.

And Carlton probably wanted me to go back into the lion's den that had my face on the "Wanted: Dead" posters.

"ADA Carlton. What brings you here?" I asked cautiously.

"I have a dead witness," Carlton answered. "Part of my case against the Women's Health Corps."

That made my blood run cold. The WHC might have only been a tool of the warlock who ran New York City, but the cult itself had raised my first demon. So anything regarding them was in my wheelhouse. It also might involve needing to smite someone.

What I said was, "Good. I didn't think they had left any witnesses."

Carlton's head tilted back and forth, balancing his words. "Funny you should put it that way..."

I sighed. "They got to your witness?"

Carlton nodded as he lowered himself next to me in the chair. "They did. I think. For about a year, he'd been slowly getting sick. Every specialist in the city couldn't find anything wrong with him.

We had people tear his house apart in case it was something environmental ..."

"Was it?" I prompted

"You could say that. Father Freeman and some Haitian experts from Flatbush identified it as Voodoo."

"He was cursed," I concluded. "To death? Interesting. But what do you want me to do about it? Bring him back from the dead?"

Jeremy grabbed my arm and bounced in his seat like he was on a sugar high. "Of course, Daddy!"

I looked from Jeremy to Carlton. "You can't be serious."

Carlton shrugged. "Why not?"

"One, I don't know if I could even help. Two, my daughter is only a few hours old. You think I'm going to leave my wife and children right now?"

"Of course you are," my wife told me that afternoon as she held our eight-hour-old daughter.

"Say again?"

Mariel looked at me with a calm, patient smile. "Jeremy?"

Jeremy shot to his feet and stood perfectly straight, as though giving a lecture. "God does not let people die from demonic infestation or curses. The only physical harm can be what God wills. If this is a curse, and this man died from it, it's because God allowed it." He paused, frowned, and added, "Or he was involved in occult stuff. It left him open to it."

Mariel nodded. "Right." She smiled at me. "We focused on the occult for a bit while you were away." She shrugged. "There are only three books on Catholic exorcisms, anyway. But if this works? It means God wanted to draw your attention to the witness. I can't imagine it *doesn't* lead you to something else. It's either going to be a two-week assignment or two days. Go. Be Secret Agent Saint. Come back to us. Got it?"

I sighed. "Yes, boss." I looked at Jeremy. "Watch after your mother while I'm gone."

Jeremy nodded. "Duh. Of course."

SAY WHAT YOU LIKE, BUT ADA WILLIAM CARLTON HAD A logical mind. Sherlock Holmes' mantra "When you have eliminated all which is impossible, then whatever remains, however improbable, must be the truth" took on a whole new light when the supernatural was no longer considered "impossible."

Before the witness, Julian Thompson, died in Carlton's office, Carlton had figured out ahead of time that Thompson had been cursed. Father Freeman had helped with the research, as well as discussing probable remedies. This included, well, me.

Carlton had gotten Julian Thompson on ice in short order. When Thompson died not four feet away from the ADA, Carlton called Sinead Holland—the only ME who knew my secret and knew that there was always an alternate hypothesis. She would work with Carlton, who didn't want Thompson in the system... It would look funny if he were registered "deceased" if, by some miracle, I had raised him from the dead. Holland could hold off being put into a system for a while. She was backed up a bit, so if he was discovered, it could have been passed off as an innocent clerical error. This showed a lot of foresight on Carlton and Holland's part. This meant that there was no evidence of his death in the first place.

So no one batted an eye when Julian Thompson walked into the courtroom three days later after I had raised him from the dead. All I had to do was pray for an hour and say, "Please."

Okay, to be honest, two people had more than batted an eye.

Those people who murdered him the first time were somewhat taken aback. Carlton would later elaborate in a 5,000-word letter that two of the defendants died of a heart attack in the courtroom. Holland would remark on the coincidence that Thompson had also died of a heart attack.

Julian Thompson had personally witnessed an element of the Women's Health Corps cult that I hadn't been made aware of. After all, I just caught them; I wasn't that involved in the prosecution (which was a good thing, since I would have been hard-pressed to explain that I had thrown the Deputy Mayor into the fire pit at the crime scene, only to have later witnessed my partner burning him down to the ground with thermite and other chemicals ... only to have met him *again* in London a few months later. And that was only one of the problems I would have had to explain under oath).

Julian Thompson was a longshoreman at one of the many piers around the greater New York area. He had been the witness to a human trafficking operation.

Thompson testified that he had done a lot of his own research on what the WHC had been up to. What did an abortion clinic chain need from Europe? He hadn't witnessed anything directly for months; he just found it curious. When the big story about my takedown of the WHC hit the papers, Thompson took it upon himself to open the latest WHC container.

Luckily for the sixty Europeans crammed inside, Thompson hadn't waited.

The human trafficking network had not been managed by the WHC, or even by their boss, the warlock, or even their consultant, the Voodoo man. They had been part of Fowler Industries, out of Europe. The origin of the containers had been Germany.

Unfortunately for the prosecution, Lord and Lady Fowler of the UK had gone missing. I refrained from explaining that the last time I had seen the Fowlers, they were on fire and being sucked into an artifact that may have ripped their souls from their bodies.

Had I been in the courtroom, I might have flipped out, screaming, *"Is everything going to come back to haunt me?"*

As it so happened, three minutes after Thompson rose from the autopsy table and told me his tale, I was booked on a plane to Europe, courtesy of the Vatican.

I called Auxiliary Bishop Xavier O'Brien, my contact with the Vatican's operations, and he told me, "You're already booked on a first class trip out of New York. I called your wife first, and she told me where you are."

I stopped, looked at the phone, and said, "How did you know I would find something?"

"You did?" XO asked. "That's good to know. I hope it leads you to Germany. Because we have a lead. By the way, your wife had a message in case you couldn't get to the phone before you left."

"And that is?"

"Quote 'I've got mom and your brother around. Go save the world.' End quote."

EUROPE

Adara screamed as she was dragged out from under her chair. The kidnapper loomed over her as Adara was raised right off the bus floor.

It was a woman. A stunning, darkly beautiful woman with blood-red stiletto boots and hair that looked like it was on fire.

"My, aren't you the tasty looking one?" she said. She licked her lips with her exceptionally long tongue. Adara knew something was wrong, but it didn't click until the kidnapper licked her lips again.

Her tongue was forked.

Adara screamed. Her kidnapper rolled her eyes and strode out of the bus, carrying Adara by the ankle in one hand. Off to the side of the road, a massive eighteen-wheeler waited. The men opened up the back of the truck, and Adara was hurled in like a sack of flour. Adara had fallen enough times in her life that she knew she had to roll with the landing.

The door slammed shut, leaving all of them in complete darkness.

The engine roared to life like a bear, the rumbling shaking Adara down to her ribs.

A hand touched hers in the darkness.

"It's okay," a voice gently says, "I'm Lena."

3 / STURM UND DRANG

I arrived in Germany in time for the dark and stormy night.

Unlike in London, when I arrived in Munich, there was more than one priest at Arrivals. There were dozens. Munich is known for many things in the 21st century. But more historically interesting is that it's the capital of the German state of Bavaria. Bavaria is to Germany as Texas is to the United States. When crossing the border, the signs there are not "Welcome to Germany," but "Welcome to Bavaria." It is also exceedingly Catholic. The first religion in Munich is "unaffiliated," the second is Catholic. When you consider what's been happening to Europe for the last few centuries, this is a borderline miracle. It's also home to the Glockenspiel, which is what would happen if Rube Goldberg had created the world's most elaborate cuckoo clock. For the drinking crowd, Munich is home to Oktoberfest.

But the flocks of priests made it hard to find *my* priest.

After two or three minutes of searching, I found Father Michael Pearson. You could easily forgive me for easily overlooking him, as he was terribly average. He was of medium height, with a sturdy build. The build was deceptive since I had seen him drop people in hand-to-hand combat. Pearson wore typical black-on-black-on black for his pants, shirt, and jacket. He was bald, mid-forties, with a closely-cropped brown beard. His eyes were brown and warm and friendly, hidden behind glasses with black frames so thick they looked like they had been borrowed from Clark Kent.

"Hello, Detective," he said in his easy British accent. I could never narrow down where it was from, but it was less London and more rural. It wasn't strictly from "the North," since Yorkshire accents were fairly distinctive. "Pleasant trip?"

I shrugged. "Close enough. How bad is it out there?"

Lightning cracked outside, followed by a thunderclap that vibrated my ribs.

Pearson shrugged. "I've seen worse."

We made it into the car from the local parish. The rain pelted the roof so hard it sounded more like hail. The windows looked like a constant river.

"So, what was your lead?" I asked.

Pearson leaned back in the chair. "Missing persons have shot up in the past month. We backtracked it and reverse engineered the progression. Several of the suspects are from a refugee program that Fowler donated to. You?"

I explained, and Pearson sighed. "Lovely. Does America ever *finish* trials? I would have thought that would have been done already."

I raised a brow. "Yes. But unlike the UK, we don't arrest citizens for speaking the truth in public, so we can afford to spend time on real crimes."

Pearson shrugged. "True enough."

"Where are we going to start?"

"Several of the parishioners who disappeared were last seen at a club. And the suspects mentioned? They're taxi drivers where people come in, but they don't come out."

I frowned. It was a similar setup to something they had used in

Rotherham, a town in the UK where there had been a "grooming gang" for thirty years—women and girls were disappeared into the sex trafficking ring and never seen again, and many of them were taken by their taxi drivers. In that case, the ring had been protected by a politically-correct culture that wouldn't dare look at Muslims cross-eyed, as well as a city police force that was on the take.

"I'm guessing we don't have a tactical team to raid the club?"

"Just you and me, and ... I have something to give you." Pearson reached into his pants pocket, lifting his butt off of the chair to reach deep enough. He came up with a ring. It looked like a college ring, with a similarly large jewel in the center. Though in this case, the jewel looked like a multi-faceted rose cut diamond. It was set in a black and silver ring. It was in my size.

"Um ... thanks?" I asked as I took it.

"You're welcome."

I held the ring close to my eye, turning towards the window so I could get a better look at it. Like a college ring, it had two emblems, one on either side of the jewel. One side was the Crusader Cross of Jerusalem—a cross with four other crosses, one in each quarter of the primary cross. The other emblem was a shield, like a family crest, in front of the crossed keys and papal crown on the Vatican flag ... the shield looked like it had an inverted sword on it, forming a cross.

"I know the cross. What's the other side?"

"The coat of arms for the Swiss guards. The shield displays the coat of arms for the current Pope."

I nodded solemnly. Pope Pius XIII was not a man who you wanted to mess with. And the crusader motif was very, very him. "Big flipping diamond, isn't it?"

"It's a piece of the Soul Stone," Pearson explained.

The bottom fell out of my stomach. "You what?"

The Soul Stone had been a prehistorical artifact that had

nearly left London a smoldering hole in the ground. Pearson and I had only stopped it because a host of angels clambered to our side and kicked the ever-loving stuffing out of a horde of Jihadists. The best guess of the "top men" at the Vatican was that the Soul Stone had been around before Abraham, in a time before polytheism, when monotheism was a natural, instinctive idea. And it had been given to the people of the first dynasty Egypt by ... something big, scary, and powerful that would later be misinterpreted as Anubis. It was even inscribed (embedded, really) with runes that were both instructions and a warning: use the stone for good, everything's cool ... misuse it at your peril. Obviously, someone had not taken the warning seriously, since the original capital of Egypt's first dynasty had been wiped off the face of the planet.

What part of "Thou shalt not FUCK with the Lord Thy God" do you not understand?

"First of all, how?" I asked. "You didn't cut it."

Pearson shrugged. "We dug up a Dominican monk who had simply amazing focus. He willed the stone off in the dimensions we needed."

I nodded. It was similar to how the Jihadists had willed off flakes from the stone. The Vatican brain trust just needed to do it once, with a larger piece. Though to get exact dimensions needed a lot more finesse.

"Second, *why?*" I snapped. "This is like giving me a grenade launcher and telling me to play in a crowded theater."

Pearson rolled his eyes. "Hardly. We figure you should have a supernatural weapon if these things are going to keep coming after you."

"Uh huh. Right." I held it up between us. "What's the difference between this and magic?"

"Magic thinks that you, the spell caster, are the source of the spell." He tapped the diamond in the ring. "*This* comes from a time when giants walked the Earth, and angels handed gifts to men. Is it magic if you weaponize the Ark of the Covenant? Or the Staff of Aaron?"

Pearson sighed and kept talking. "We know that the money trail from the Fowlers goes to Berlin, but it's gotten moved around a lot. But we know a large portion of them are coming through Bavaria since the majority of missing girls have been from here for the past three months. We won't even discuss the missing persons who may be coming in from elsewhere in Europe."

I cocked my head. I still held the Soul Ring, but I slipped it in my pocket. I didn't want to try putting it on yet. "Why is that?

Pearson groaned. "It's the Continent. It's a mess. You can kidnap a girl in France and get her to Minsk before 24 hours pass by, depending on the traffic. And good luck running it past Interpol. The flipping EU thought that they would be the United States of Europe, they barely ended up with the UN of Europe, and their Europol people are about as effective as the Blue Helmets, who are either committing genocide or on cigarette break while genocide happens around them."

"And in this case?"

"We go into the club. We see what we can find out. We wing it from there."

THE RUMBLING OF THE TRUCK SEEMED ENDLESS. IT ONLY felt like it had been going on forever. The truck pulled to a stop from time to time, but the engine's roar never ceased. Between the perfect dark inside of the truck and the constant growl, Adara could have easily imagined it being the inside of a lion.

"Lena, are you awake?" Adara whispered.

Lena didn't say anything for a long moment. Adara couldn't see her but imagined what Lena might have been thinking. Of course, Lena was awake. Who could sleep with the truck's engine so close and a container so cramped?

"Yes."

"Miss Feder still won't wake up."

Lena said nothing for a moment. "She's not well. Some Doctors call it catatonia."

It was Adara's turn to say nothing. Lena had explained on the way that she had seen plenty of doctors at her orphanage. Lena suspected that it was one of the doctors who had sold her to these men. Because Lena was worse than an orphan—she was a *strange* orphan. And who wanted a strange little girl? Lena had been raised by nuns, but the EU gave Poland a hard time about religious-run orphanages. That meant Lena had to go into the hands of "charity" homes run by secular NGOs. The people who suggested the EU impose regulations like that on Poland were the same people who ran the NGO. Lena had heard the names often enough: "Fowler" and "Toynbee."

But Lena had seen a lot of doctors as a result. Some of these doctors had had accidents when they treated her poorly. Adara wondered what Lena meant, and Lena, without hearing Adara ask it aloud, said, "I thought bad things at them, and they happened."

Adara had two simultaneous thoughts—that Lena was a little scary, and that scary might be a really good thing in this instance. Lena put an arm around her protectively, and they both slept for the first time since they were kidnapped.

But now, they were awake, the engine roaring, and sleep was impossible. Adara was certain that her bus would be missed, but how long would that take? And how long would it take to organize a search between countries? Lena was Polish. Adara was Czech. Some of the others were Russian. Though who would be crazy enough to kidnap Russians? Russia didn't like it when that happened.

"Heretics," Lena told Adara. "Heretics would do that."

Again, Adara wondered how Lena did that. This time, Lena did not answer her unspoken thought. Was it because Lena couldn't hear it, or because Lena just didn't want to answer?

Lena ruffled Adara's hair.

The truck slowed to a stop again. The doors opened and flooded the cabin with light. Adara was blinded and forced to look away. As her eyes adjusted, she saw Lena for the first time. Lena was an older girl, a whole thirteen years old. She was really pretty, as pretty as her voice. That was easily discernible even through the messy hair, which formed a gold curtain around her face. Lena had bright blue eyes and high cheekbones. It must have been a Polish thing.

The tall woman with the scary looks stepped onto the truck, framed by the doorway, and backlit by the floodlights. But the shadow she cast was certainly female. Her eyes flicked to life, lit from the inside. They were a catlike green, complete with a vertical slit for a pupil. The gaze was something she had seen in documentaries about big hunting cats.

Before, Adara had merely concluded that their kidnapper was inhuman. Now she was certain that the kidnapper was another species entirely.

The kidnapper's eyes lit on Miss Feder. She smiled like she was going in for the kill. The monster pointed. The men laughed, hopped into the truck, and grabbed Feder.

Miss Feder snapped alert as though awakened from a trance. She screamed. The men laughed and spoke to each other in a language Adara didn't know—and she knew German, Czech, Yiddish, Polish, and Russian.

Miss Feder thrashed and screamed as she was taken off the truck.

The woman smiled at the rest of the prisoners...and her eyes came to rest on Lena and Adara before she hopped off the back of the truck. At her command, the door slid down, leaving only a few inches open on the bottom, providing plenty of light... And allowing all of them to hear Miss Feder's screams.

Adara leaned closer to Lena, afraid of what would happen if anyone heard her. "What was that? What did she say?"

" 'Get her ready,' " Lena said, " 'She's already halfway broken.' "

Adara blinked, confused. "You understood what they said?"

Lena shook her head slowly. "I understood *her*."

"And at the end?"

"Let them listen."

Then Miss Feder's screams began in earnest.

4 / NIGHT MOVES

A lot of the money from Lord Fowler and Lady Toynbee went to, of all places, a night club for "refugees" called Ficken.

I stood across the street from the nightclub, underneath the awning of a bakery. I looked over the neon lights and gawked at how truly gaudy this was. It was worse than anything I had ever seen out of Las Vegas or Times Square. It had neon signs, neon trim, all in colors of pink, blue, green and yellow.

To say it was an outlier is underestimating the matter. From what I could see of Munich in the dark, it was very pretty. The architecture ran the gamut from medieval to ultra-modern. It's strange imagining that the Gothic Cathedral and the headquarters of BMW shared the same city. But every building I noted obviously showed *effort*. They *liked* architecture and took pride in looking good. This was a city that had been bombed fairly heavily in World War II, and the reconstruction effort tried to reconstruct what had been. Only the most recent construction looked extremely new. But it all looked *good*. I had to restrain myself from playing tourist.

This place? This looked like a concrete bunker someone tried to dress up to look like a 1970s pimp.

"How in Hell is this supposed to be a refugee thing?" I asked. "It looks more like a sex club."

Father Pearson stood next to me, his collar covered by his raincoat. "It probably is. That's why it's so far on the outskirts of the city. Even in the strange culture of Germany, when it comes to sex, this is fairly backwater. As for *refugees* ... Supposedly, it's where refugees can mingle among their own and feel comfortable. In reality..."

Pearson drifted off. I had noted the people coming in and the people being dropped off in taxis. The taxi drivers and the bouncers were clearly Middle Eastern.

"It's bait," I concluded.

"Right. Drugs and drinking in a noisy, hard-to-see environment means that its easy to kidnap attendees."

I grimaced, trying to reconcile this with data I'd already had. "This is the country that had rape gangs roving the streets freely for a New Year's Eve, isn't it?"

Pearson dismissively waved his hand. His face clearly expressed disgust with the situation, and his tone was mocking. "Oh, but that was Cologne! And Hamburg! Surely that could never happen *here*." He spat on the sidewalk. "And of the *thousands* of reported rapes, the German government only prosecuted a few hundred. I suspect because they couldn't cover them up. Dear God, I feel like even a *casual* knowledge of history is more about making me watch people do the same exact stupid bollocks over and over again."

"Probably." I gave him a glance. "How are you an expert in local problem spots? I half-expected another priest to be my partner on this one. You told me you had a degree in archaeology."

"I do. But XO thought that we worked well together. And priests with my skill set are rare."

I didn't ask for further information. I was almost afraid to ask.

"Are we going in or not?"

Pearson sighed. "Come on, let's get it over with."

We walked up to the two bouncers. I caught only the faintest whiff of sin off them.

One of these days, I'll be able to tell one scent of sin over another.

The bouncers looked us up and down and exchanged a glance. One shook his head at the other, ready to deny us entry. I was big, but they were bigger.

I didn't wait for their little nonverbal powwow to be over before I kicked the knee of my bouncer sideways, breaking it. He screamed out as he landed on the bad knee. I grabbed his head in both hands and rammed it into the wall behind him.

His buddy turned to engage me, and Pearson kicked out his knee from behind him, bringing him down. It made it easier for me to kick him in the face with the sole of my boot.

"After you," Pearson said, waving me into the club.

I entered the club and was hit with the true source of the smell —the club itself. The scene was one part dance club and one part the second circle of Hell, with techno music. Fog machines poured mist from the floor and the ceiling. Laser beams flashed in beat to the music and the strobe lights. Someone was trying to induce a seizure. One can easily tell jokes about how modern "dancing" was more like vertical, clothed, mutual masturbation. This wasn't even a joke, since most of the patrons were in a state of undress, going from shirtless to just plain naked.

In the ride on the way over, we had a discussion on plenty of things. One of which was attire. Wouldn't we stand out in long raincoats in the middle of a nightclub? I needn't have worried.

Pearson explained that Ficken is German for "fuck." And perverts in raincoats were not out of place there. I was still too dressed in my shirt and tie, and yet I wasn't dressed enough. Most of the patrons were naked, but what clothing I saw on people ranged from nightclub chic to expensive business attire.

I would have stood out in the club ... if anyone paid attention.

The club went up several stories. The upper levels were rings around the main dance floor ... only no one was dancing. Many of them disappeared into the floor, consumed by the mist from the fog machine.

I tapped Pearson on the shoulder and pointed up. He nodded and pointed to the bar.

I would be on overwatch on the third floor. Pearson would be on the first floor. Between the two of us, we should be able to catch someone being dragged out against their will.

I took the stairs to the third floor. If the dance floor was a public orgy, I was afraid to imagine what they were doing in the elevators. I made it to the third floor without incident. Only *half* of these patrons were in the middle of screwing their brains out. The other half were at booths watching the fun.

If I sound judgmental, I am. Half the club wasn't married. The half that was weren't screwing with their own wives. Seriously, if you're going to have sex in public, be with your own wife. The scene itself was a turnoff, I had the sudden urge to go home and cuddle with Mariel—and at that moment, I hadn't been able to do more with Mariel than cuddle for several months, so that tells you how much the sights and sounds turned me off.

I found a part of the rail that overlooked the main floor. I picked and leaped my way over the bodies rolling on the floor to make it there. The first hand that grabbed for me was a delicate one and easily pulled away from. The second was a man's, and I kicked out. The third set was one of each. I had had enough and stomped down with my free foot. I didn't feel the crunch of bones, but I definitely connected. And one of them called out "Yes! Do that again!"

I rolled my eyes and kept going to the rail.

The orgy laid out before me was an impressive spectacle, if one didn't mind something from the mind of Caligula ... or was it just that terrible movie with Malcolm McDowell? Either way, it was something out of a nightmare where sex started to look like something out of a Bosch hellscape. The clawing and thrashing were animalistic ... which would be fine if blood weren't being drawn more often than not.

Wait, was it that bad when I entered?

It got worse as the seconds ticked by. Scratching and hair pulling were one thing, but the biting began. Then the clawing.

It's all fun and games until the maenads tear you apart.

I took a deep breath. The stench wasn't all that distinctive from what I had smelled on other occasions. One would think that sex would smell different than murder and would smell different than the manifestation of a full demon.

From behind me came a low, seductive voice. "Hello, handsome."

Not expecting English (and worried that someone knew who I was), I turned around. Standing there was a tall redhead of unusually well-developed physique. She ... might have been legal. Her hourglass figure and long waist were on full display—also that she was a natural redhead.

Her face was a starved heart shape—round on top but with narrow cheeks and a sharp little chin that ended too quickly. The bottom of her face was balanced by full sensuous lips. Her large luminous green eyes sparked with hunger or passion, take your pick.

"*Guten tag,*" I said, exhausting my German.

"I know you're American," she said, fingering my tie. She smiled coyly as she reached for my tie and felt it up, stroking it. Her deep green eyes stared into mine. "I'm Jayden."

"I'm Tom," I gasped out, my mouth suddenly dry.

Jayden laughed. "Don't worry, you're nothing new." She tapped her index fingernail and slid down my tie. "Lonely American." Her finger slid over my belt and over to my wedding ring. "Far from the wife."

She flicked the tip of her finger over the back of my hand. I felt shocks up my arm, stiffening my spine and other parts of me. I felt my IQ slipping away as my arousal spiked. My vision blurred around the edges as it tunneled on her and only her. Tingles ran all over my body. Above the smell of sin, I could smell her. She set my heart racing. My breathing became heavy, as though I had run a race. My blood pulsed and throbbed all over. Even my hands itched to reach for her...

Except for the scars on my hands. And all of my other scars. The scars were fine, no tingling at all.

Glory be to the Father and to the Son and to the Holy Spirit. As it was, in the beginning, is now and ever shall be, world without end, Amen.

My head cleared, my vision became 20/20, and my pulse calmed.

I wasn't the only one who changed.

Jayden's eyes glowed. The pupil became a verticle slit, like a cat. A big cat. Her canines had grown just a little bit more, stopping just short of fangs. Her fingernails had grown into claws. Her skin had grown scales, covering her from neck to toe, strangely making her more modest. Her hair had gone from fire engine red to blood red.

"One of *you!*" she spat.

Jayden, whatever she was, reared back with her claws.

I shot both of my hands forward. My left arm slammed against her inner arm, just below the elbow so I could check her swing. My right fist drove through her face, knocking her head back.

It was tempting to grapple with her and weigh her down. If she were a human being, I would do just that. But I wasn't going to test her strength or how sharp her nails were. The last thing I needed was razor sharp, poison-filled claws ripping out a chunk of my hip.

I grabbed her right wrist with my left hand and the shoulder with my right. I stepped back with my right foot and swung her around, throwing her into the wall. Jayden bounced off the wall into my left roundhouse. She spun around in a half-turn. I kicked her left hip with the heel of my boot, causing her body to buckle and turn. With her back to me, I grabbed Jayden by her hip and her neck and hurled her over the railing.

Jayden went flying.

Then Jayden sprouted two bat wings and started flying for real.

She circled back, her hands filled with fire. She shrieked like a banshee.

The music cut out. Everyone in the club stopped their sex games and turned to the monster. Instead of fleeing in terror, a low growl filled the club, coming from every throat.

It took only a second to piece together what was happening. Jayden's effect on me meant she was a succubus. Everyone having sex in the club meant that they fed her and put themselves under her sway.

Which meant that I either had to break her hold on them or kill everybody in the night club before they tore me apart.

I whirled around and decked the first guy nearest me. I plowed into the club goers, driving into them and through them. I figured it would be better with my back to the wall than my back to the succubus.

The formerly sex-mad nightclub patrons reached out and grabbed for me. Some for my arms and others for my ankles. A grab to the wrist was a quick twist of the arm so that the narrow end of the wrist could punch through the opening in the grip—followed by an elbow to the face. A grab with the opposite hand became a twist of the hips to shoot out of the grip and to deliver a punch to the face. A two-handed grip was an excuse for me to stomp on a naked instep with my iron-toed boot and deliver a head butt to the face. A grab for my ankle was meant to trip me but allowed me to kick someone in the head—again, iron-toed boot. One tried to grab my groin, but that was deflected with a quick hip twist.

A naked man slammed into me from the left. I went with the blow, swinging my left side around while my right foot stayed planted and pivoted. The effect was matador and bull, where he kept running past me. Another one slammed into me from the right, and that caused me to face-plant into the floor.

Get up, or you're toast.

I pushed off of the floor and got my feet under me before everyone within spitting distance jumped on top of me, piling on.

Hail Mary, full of Grace ... ack! Please hold.

With a scream of exertion, I pushed up reared back with a bellow as I straightened up and threw off the clingers. The ones who fell before me seemed stunned as they hit the ground. They tried to get up, and I stomped on the chest of one of them and kicked the other in the face as I pushed through.

I dug into my pocket as I threw myself against the wall, back first. Then I pulled out my secret weapon: a small atomizer. I sprayed the area ahead of me before anyone could rush me. The first person to reach me fell down. She screamed and writhed in agony. Three other people tried to get to me, and they also ran straight into the mist.

Several months ago, on our way from London to Rome, Pearson and I had discussed several things. One of which was a weapons kit that the Vatican could assemble for me. Part of that discussion inspired someone in Rome to give me the Soul Ring ... which was still in my pants pocket. In the car, Pearson gave me my kit. Atomizers of holy water, vials of holy oil, packets of holy salt, and a deck of Mass cards.

Believe it or not, everything, including the salt, is real *and* effective against demons.

The holy water I had sprayed in front of me had severed the club-goers connection to "Jayden." Apparently, it hurt.

Jayden screamed and opened fire—literally. Streams of fire flew from her palms and punched through several of her minions like they weren't even there. I sprayed some more in front of me and hit the ground.

The flames had hit the mist of holy water and stopped, held off by the spray.

I rolled out of the line of fire, onto my feet and charged off to the side, keeping one of the support walls between me and the succubus.

I reached my free hand into my pocket when Jayden swooped in and flew straight at my face with a fist full of fire.

I threw the holy salt packet from my pocket straight into her face. She screamed and blocked it with her fiery fist. The salt quenched the flames in her hand, and she dropped to the floor.

I promptly kicked her in the stomach. She pushed off the floor with the blow and rolled to her feet. She seemed disoriented but still assumed a wide, low stance, like a classical wrestler.

First, I sprayed my hands with the atomizer, then the area in front of me, and Jayden growled, bursting back. She grabbed a table, ripped off the top, and hurled it at me. I dropped flat and rolled under it as it embedded itself in the wall. I popped up from the floor and drove an uppercut into Jayden. The blow rocked her. I recoiled a hair faster than Jayden's claw. Otherwise I would have lost my arm just below the wrist.

I shot forward with both of my arms in front of me up in a block, checking her arm against her body. I thrust my fingers into her eyes. It wasn't a particularly hard jab. My fingernails weren't particularly long.

However, those fingers were covered in holy water.

Jayden shrieked and shoved me away... with the arm I had checked. Even though I had her arm pinned, with no leverage, she threw me back against the wall, above the table she'd thrown at me. I landed on the table, and it held.

I was seized by a collection of Jayden's thralls. They grabbed my wrists and ankles. Jayden had decided that I had too many holy weapons to strike her with, so the thralls were a safer bet. One of them pried open my fingers to get at the atomizer and tossed it on the floor.

They held me tightly. I thrashed against them, but there were three of them on each arm. Jayden took a moment but was back on her feet and staring straight at me. There was no sign of damage from the holy water, but for all I knew, she had ripped off and regrown her entire face when I wasn't looking.

"You'll pay for this!" Jayden growled, her voice no longer human. "And I'll *make* you enjoy it." She didn't smile; she bared her teeth. Each tooth had become sharper, like a narrow shark tooth. Her bat wings flared out. She walked towards me in a strut that would have been seductive, if she weren't a demon from Hell.

Jayden placed her hand flat on my chest and leaned over me. My body reacted positively, despite the terror I felt.

My physiology must be very confused right now.

In a low, seductive voice, Jayden said, "I want you to appreciate what's going to happen to you. This is a special case for you. First, my venom will seep into your veins." Her hand dragged along my shirt, nails putting only a slight pressure on my chest without breaking the skin. "You'll be so driven by lust, you'll only be good as a toy. In a few minutes, you'll be so hard, I could use your cock to break rocks." Her hand slipped over my belt. "Then I'm going to use you. I will suck the life out of you until you're an empty husk." She cupped me and smiled broadly. "Hmmm. At least, you'll make for good sport."

Her left hand gripped me. Her right hand touched my face like a caress. I quickly grasped for a half-remembered prayer by St. Thomas Aquinas.

Dearest Jesus! I pray You to defend, with Your grace, chastity, and purity in my soul as well as in my body. And if I have ever received through my senses any impression that could stain my chastity and purity, may You, Who are the Supreme Lord of all my powers, take it from me, that I may with an immaculate heart advance in Your love and service, offering myself chaste all the days of my life on the most pure altar of Your Divinity. Amen.

Jayden smiled and leaned closer. "You'll never defeat my master. Asmodeus will rise, and you can do nothing against him."

Asmodeus?

She scratched me.

Jayden winced a little and pulled her hand back from my face. The tip of a claw was cut off at the tip, still smoking. We exchanged a confused look for a moment. Neither one of us knew what had happened. Then it occurred to me that when I faced down a warlock, my blood burned away the living shadows he had weaponized. Apparently, it burned away more substantial evil, too.

Jayden rolled her eyes. Her voice became flat and annoyed. "Or I can just rip your dick off and let you bleed to death. That works too."

"Pardon me!" a chipper voice called out.

Jayden and all of the thralls turned towards the stairs. Father Pearson was by the door and waved at the group as he walked towards us. He put both hands behind him as he approached us.

"Hello!" he chirped. "I'm Father Michael Pearson. Am I interrupting this party, or can anyone join in?"

Jayden didn't release her grip on me, and I was very, very careful not to make any sudden movements. She smiled. "*Well now,*" she practically purred. "I haven't had one of *you* for a few years."

Pearson nodded with a smile. "Indeed. Good to know."

Jayden nodded at me. "Is he one of yours?"

"Isn't everyone here?" Pearson asked. He stopped two strides away from Jayden. "These are my sheep."

Jayden smiled. "You've come to bargain?"

Pearson's smile went flat and his eyes went cold. "A shepherd doesn't bargain with wolves. We kill them."

Jayden's smile gave way to a growl. "In which case, I—"

A scream ripped through the nightclub. They came from above and below us. Howls of pain and despair came from all over the nightclub. Jayden looked away from Pearson for a split second, confused by the sudden cries.

Pearson shot his hands forwards from behind his back, throwing fistfuls of holy salts all over Jayden, the thralls, and me. The thralls screamed and fell back, releasing me. Jayden used both hands to cover her head, freeing me entirely. I kicked off the table, sliding to the floor, and swept up the atomizer, unbroken.

Pearson burst in, smacking Jayden across the face, the crystals of holy salt still clinging to his hands. He grabbed her forehead and cried out, "Mary, Mother most pure, and Joseph, chaste guardian of the Virgin, to you I entrust the purity of my soul and body. I earnestly wish to be pure in thought, word, and deed in imitation of your own holy purity. Obtain for me a deep sense of modesty. Protect my eyes, the windows of my soul, from anything that might dim the luster of a heart that must mirror only Christ-like purity. And seal my heart forever against the suggestions of sinful pleasures—"

Jayden screamed and pushed Pearson away, so hard he slid across the floor.

I followed up by spraying her in the face with the holy water. She shrieked in pain and hurled herself past me, over the railing, and spread her wings to fly away. She flew up, through the fog machines pouring out mist to the ceiling.

I grabbed Pearson and helped him to his feet. He said, "Not over yet."

Jayden's scream did not sound human, more like something from Godzilla. I turned in time to watch her fall from the ceiling and into the floor covered in fog. She continued to scream as though she were continually being set on fire. Her voice rose above the others in the night club, who were also screaming the pains of the damned.

"What the—"

Pearson gave a simple laugh. "While everyone was interested

in killing you, no one noticed as I blessed all the water in the fog machines."

Jayden leaped from the floor onto the bar. Her entire body looked like it had been scarred with acid. Her hair had been burned off. She looked more like a reptile than anything else.

Jayden looked up at the railing, at Pearson and at me, and glared. She hissed, again like a large cat, and this time, she let out a roar that shook the building.

All of the doors for the night club kicked in. Gunmen swarmed the club, flooding the floor like the fog had.

Jayden pointed up at us and shrieked. And all the gunmen swung their guns up to us and opened fire.

Adara cuddled closer to Lena, and the older girl held her tight. Outside the truck, even over the roar of the engine, came screaming. Horrible screaming. Endless screaming. It sounded like the suffering souls of the damned were right outside. Every so often, there was the cry of something terrible.

"What do you think it is?" Adara asked.

Lena said nothing for a long moment. "They're fighting something."

Adara perked up. Someone was fighting their kidnappers? "That's great. They're good guys, right?"

"I think so. They're beating up our bad guys."

"You think these people will find us?"

Lena frowned. "Maybe."

Lena's attention turned to the door. Her brows furrowed, and her lips pursed as she concentrated on it.

Adara watched Lena for a moment. "What are you doing?"

"I'm getting mad at the door."

Adara frowned. Lena had told her that bad things happened when she was upset or angry. "You think that's going to work?"

Lena's posture and face didn't change. "Maybe."

"Think about the scary woman."

The door to the container BANGED. A dent appeared in the door.

Adara blinked. It worked. Had it worked? "How about the men with guns?"

BANG.

The dent grew deeper.

Adara grew sad as her mind sought something else. She meekly said, "Miss Feder?"

The back door of the truck blew off of its hinges.

The men with guns swarmed in front of the truck door, searching for what happened.

Lena stood up, still angry. "You hurt us."

The men lowered their guns. It was just a little girl, after all.

Then Lena showed them how mad she was.

PEARSON AND I FELL BACK AS THE AUTOMATIC FIRE SWEPT AT us like a wave. Clubgoers freed from the succubus' thrall scattered as the gunfire broke out. Many headed for the front door without even stopping for clothing. I didn't blame them.

While I didn't know the response time for the cops of Munich, if it were like the bad areas of New York, it might take them as long as fifteen minutes to get to the club. Thirty minutes if they were particularly disdainful of the area. Then again, with all the gunfire, they might be here in five minutes if they were worried about terrorism.

However, that was still plenty of time for the gunmen to ventilate the both of us. The elevator dinged behind me. My head whipped around. Three of the gunmen were already upon us. I scrambled and charged the door. The doors slid open. The three gunmen had their AK-47s up to their shoulders. I came in low, under the barrels, and snapped up, slamming the three of them against the elevator's back wall. My shoulders, arms, and body kept the muzzles pointed towards the ceiling, far too close to their own faces for the gunmen to try pulling the trigger.

Pearson darted into the elevator before the doors could close. He grabbed the AK on my far right, taking it by the butt and the barrel, yanking it down and away from the gunman who owned it. Pearson reared back and slammed the butt of the gun into its owner's head, as though trying to pound a nail into the elevator wall.

Now that I didn't have to worry about three gunmen, just two, I grabbed the men I had pinned by the sides of their heads and proceeded to smash them together. Two, three, four times. Then they slumped down.

I reached back for the grip of the elevator and held it before the doors closed. "Hit the emergency button."

Pearson did so without asking why. Elevators would be a box that would get us killed. He handed me the AK he'd recovered. "I'll collect the others."

I nodded, took the rifle, and wheeled off the elevator, checking the balcony before coming out. Since we were on the third floor, it would take a minute to get everyone. Thankfully, there was only one set of stairs that went up to this level.

I tried to think of a ready prayer, but all I could think of was the man in the army uniform in London, who might have been Michael the Archangel himself.

Saint Michael, heaven's glorious commissioner of police, who once so neatly and successfully cleared God's premises of all undesirables, look with kindly and professional eyes on your earthly force. Give us cool heads, stout hearts, and an uncanny flair for investigation and wise judgment. Make us the terror of burglars, the friend of children and law-abiding citizens, kind to strangers, polite to bores, strict with law-breakers, and impervious to temptations.

You know, Saint Michael, from your own experiences with the devil, that the police officer's lot on earth is not always a happy one; but may your sense of duty that so pleased God, your hard knocks that so surprised the devil, and your angelic self-control give us inspiration. And when we lay down our night sticks, enroll us in your heavenly force, where we will be as proud to guard the throne of God as we have been to guard the city of all the people. Amen.

"Hey, Michael," I muttered. "You want to see me do my John Wick impression?"

I darted forward, the rifle at my shoulder, aimed at the stairs. I had switched to single fire. I would need the ammunition.

I came to the stairs and kept my eyes down the staircase as I walked around it and the glass rail and banister that kept people from falling down drunk onto the stairs. There was nothing that said I had to play fair with the forces of darkness. These people were in league with a succubus. They had walked through the holy water mist and hadn't changed their minds. They hadn't fled the club when a connection *should* have been severed. They knew what Jayden was, and they knew what was being done here.

I was almost certainly a dead man. My main hope was that I would stop enough of them so that Pearson could get out alive when the fighting was over.

The gunmen made it to the bottom step. Their gaze was focused on the stairs ahead of them. If they had real-world military or law enforcement training, they would look up. Hell, if they had played video games, they would have looked up.

I looked down and watched them come up. The leader's head was level with the top step when I opened fire. I fired one, catching him in the back of the head.

The entire formation stopped and dropped into a crouch, which suited me just fine as I kept firing. I was so close to them, I didn't need careful aim. I didn't even pause as I swept down the stairs, dropping each and every one of them.

There was still movement, but they now knew where I was.

I rose and sidestepped, going from the head of the stairs to a right angle to them. Three men jeans and t-shirts clambered over their fallen comrades.

I hopped over the railing and landed right on top of them, knocking them back like bowling pins. I landed in a crouch on top of a corpse and fired into the other gunmen behind them— who had come in far too close together. I fired from a crouch on the stairs, so I was level with their heads. One. Two. Three, they fell. I pushed off of the stairs with both feet and landed on one of the men I knocked back. I knocked the wind out of him and shot the other two men I'd bowled over. Then I drove the rifle into his face like a hammer.

I leaned out from the staircase to look around the edge. More gunmen were coming.

I waited a moment, listening for their footsteps, timing how long it would take to get to me. I counted down. *Three ... two ... one!*

I sprang out from my crouch and around the stairs. Once again, I came in under a rifle, using my own AK to parry the barrel up. This put my muzzle almost into the ear of the gunman next to him. I pulled the trigger, blasting him away.

I swung the AK muzzle to the right, clipping the gunman in front of me on the ear. I wrapped my arms around him (hands still full of AK), hugging him to my body. With him trapped in place, I charged his buddies and opened fire, using him for a shield. The gunman's body vibrated with the impacts of bullets.

I slammed him into the crowd of gunmen. I tossed my now-dead shield onto a gunman to my left. I deflected the rifle in front of me to point at the gunmen on my right, and the gunman opened fire, killing his own friend. I jammed my muzzle into the gunman's throat and pulled the trigger. *Click.*

My AK was empty.

I swung the rifle into the gunman's face as though elbowing him—only I struck him with the butt of the gun. His head rocked back as I dropped my rifle. I grabbed the knife from his belt, slashed up with the blade, slicing open his stomach, and stabbed down into his collar bone. I hooked him and swung him to keep his friends from shooting me. With my left hand, I grabbed his sidearm out of his holster, pulled it out and jabbed it into the throat of the gunman on my left.

I yanked the thug in front of me and fired into his friends. Head shot front, right, then left. I cracked the leftward gunman again in the neck, pressed the muzzle to his temple, and fired. I stabbed it into the man I held and fired. The bullet went in one side and out the other.

I dropped to a crouch, narrowed my eyes as I scanned the area. When no other gunmen came up, I grabbed the fallen AK from one of the dead men, then checked the settings for single fire.

I charged for the next set of stairs (which, stupidly, were put at an opposite corner of the second floor). I swung around into the staircase and fired twice with the fresh AK, catching one gunman in the stomach. I fired a third time into his compatriot, then a fourth time into his head, keeping him down.

I swept downstairs and cleared the next floor down. No other gunmen were lying in wait for us on the first floor. Even Jayden was gone. I took a deep breath. I couldn't smell much in the way of evil. There were faint traces left, but they were just that—faint.

"Father!" I bellowed, not taking my eyes off the rifle sights. "You can bring the elevator down."

Gunshots rang from out back. "I'm moving!"

"I'll follow."

I ran into the first door into the back. It led into the kitchen, which was empty. I ran straight through, sweeping the kitchen once with the AK. I kicked through the back door, into a massive garage. The back door was wide open, and the truck's engine was still running, even though it was parked.

Four men raced to the back of the truck, their rifles high. There was already a pile of bodies at the back bumper, but they seemed interested in adding to it.

The gunmen stopped at the truck and raised their guns.

I fired first, dropping the first two. The other two swung to face me and probably would have gunned me down. Except one gunman slammed into another, as though someone gave him a hard shove. Both gunmen slammed into a wall. I gunned them both down without hesitation.

I made my way to the edge of the truck and sneaked a quick peek. Then I took a longer look.

It was a truck full of civilians. They were all young, and a collection of them were children. Everyone was dirty. The cabin smelled of body odor, excrement, and diesel. I preferred the diesel.

The one who stood out was a little blonde girl, maybe thirteen, about a year older than Jeremy. She was covered in blood and viscera and ... brains? She had bright blue eyes, and her blonde hair was strung with blood.

I raised one hand as I made a show of lowering my gun. It took me a moment to remember that there was one word that would be recognizable to most of Eastern Europe.

"Politzei! Politzei!" I called.

A smaller child, a brown-haired girl who *wasn't* covered in blood, turned to the other prisoners and started chattering to them. They cheered a little and roused themselves.

"Um ... American?"

The blonde girl didn't move any. I gently placed the gun on

the back bumper of the truck. I gave her a little finger wave. She didn't move for a moment, studying me curiously.

The little brunette poked the blonde and chattered at her in ... something Eastern European. The blonde nodded. She understood that I was a cop, the brunette told her.

I gave her a little wave. "Hi."

The door I came through opened. I looked back. It was Pearson. I looked back to the blonde and raised my index finger. "One moment." I waved Pearson over, and he came running. He slid to a stop next to me. I waved into the truck, and he looked.

"Oh my."

"How's your general knowledge of Eastern European languages?" I asked. "I think they're from all over the place, if I hear them right."

I looked at the blood-covered girl. Her eyes locked on Pearson. She smiled broadly at the sight of his collar. She flung herself at me, joyously crying, "Hussar!"

I caught her with a confused smiled. She clung to me like I was Superman, and I just got her off a ledge.

"Hussar?" I asked. "She thinks I'm the cavalry?"

Pearson looked from inside the truck to me. "Tell me you weren't."

He had a point.

Pearson pointed towards the front. "I'm going to turn off the engine."

"Good idea." I looked back to the girl in my arms. "Hi. I'm Tommy."

She smiled brightly. "I'm Lena."

I smiled. "That's a very pretty name, Lena."

The brunette charged out, stopped at the lip of the truck, crawled down, then attached herself to my leg.

Lena leaned over to whisper in my ear, "I should go down now. Adara needs me. She's just a kid, you know."

"Ah," I said seriously. I lowered Lena down, and Adara detached herself from me and clung to Lena.

The engine cut out. Pearson came out of the truck. "I think we're going to have to call this in. The police will want to know that there are some good guys on the ground over here."

The police broke in on us about ten minutes later. They had only sent three cop cars, despite that the battle must have sounded like a war to anyone who had passed by.

Much to my surprise, no one put the cuffs on me. I was the last man standing in a building full of dead people and obvious victims of human trafficking. But then, when I sat down on the loading dock, I was at one end, all of the kidnap victims on the dock next to me, with Adara and Lena holding onto me as though I were the biggest, best, armed stuffed animal that they had ever owned. The uniforms had probably presumed that I was already pinned down.

Also, I had a Catholic priest speaking for me. That might have allayed some suspicion.

From what I knew, Lena Mazur and Adara Weil were both kidnapped. Lena from her orphanage and Adara from a tour bus.

Kommissar Sebastian Berger was a Munich detective who arrived on the scene a few minutes after the uniforms had shown up. He was sharp-profiled, in late middle age, with short brown hair. He seemed very relaxed for someone who had just walked through a crime scene like that.

Berger's tired brown eyes looked over my badge. It had been

passed around from cop to cop like it was a football. He walked over to me and didn't look up when he said, "Thomas Nolan, eh?" He only then paid me a glance. Adara and Lena clinging to me brought a small smile to his face. He gestured with my badge wallet. "You have admirers, yes?"

"I guess so. Sorry for the mess."

Berger glanced back to the door leading to the club. "Normally, I would accept the apology, but not today." He looked at the girls. "Do they speak English?"

"Yes," Lena said, her face buried in my arm. "Hussar killed all the bad men."

Berger's brows arched, but he didn't comment on what she said. "You're right about that. They were *very* bad men." He met my eye. "They were so bad; three of our men have walked into this club but never walked out again."

The light dawned. The Munich cops hadn't thrown me to the ground and cuffed me because I had solved a problem they had dealt with over months. If they had gotten to the point where they had already started sending in undercover officers, then Pearson had been wrong— people had been disappearing into the club for much longer than he thought they were. They had lost personnel trying to figure out how the club operated.

Then in came the big dumb American who shot up the place like John Wayne, John Rambo, or John McClane. And I wasn't even a John.

Berger placed my badge next to me on the loading dock since both my arms were pinned by the girls. "So, Detective, would you like to tell me what brings you to our beautiful city?"

I tried to shrug, but that might dislodge the girls. "What would be easier for you? A story, or the truth?"

Kommissar Berger smiled. "Let us start with the truth. We can sanitize it for a report later."

I had always heard that any tightly-controlled culture had to have extremely creative loopholes to function. It's part of how the word "Jesuitical" came to be. It's why for every military outfit, there will be at least one guy who could "creatively request" (read: pilfer) supplies. It's part of how cop humor runs. Apparently, there was a strain of that in German culture. Or maybe that was just Bavaria.

"I'm on detachment with NYPD's intelligence division. I basically function on attachment with the Vatican as a sort of troubleshooter."

Berger's eyes flicked to Pearson, then back to me. "Ah. That explains one part of it. And the data led you here?"

I nodded. "Middle Eastern taxi drivers pick up clients to come here, and some don't make it. Some women come into the club and don't come home. All we did—" I looked to Pearson to include him in this as well "—was come here to look around. We were going to feel out the situation. We didn't expect to find ... any of this. From the orgy in there to the terrorists."

Berger nodded slowly. "Ah. Very interesting. How did the firefight start?"

"One of the people who run the club recognized me. A fight ensued. The civilians fled. Then the gunmen were called in."

Berger waved me on. "And then?"

"Depends. Did Germany ever get to see *John Wick*?"

Berger smiled. "Ah, yes. Keanu. 'Whoa.' I understand."

He pointed to the pile of bodies on the floor by the truck. The forensics on all of that was ruined. Everyone from the truck had stepped in, on, or around the dead kidnappers.

"They were dead when I got here," I told him, which was the truth. "I have no direct knowledge of what happened to them." This was also the truth.

Berger cocked his head. "How very ... precise you are in your language."

Next to me, Lena spoke up just loud enough to be heard through my coat. "I killed them with my brain."

Berger looked to Lena. "How did you do that?"

Lena looked out at him. "I thought bad things at them and that happened."

Berger nodded slowly. "Uh. Huh." He looked at the pile of bodies, chewing the inside of his lip. He looked back to the three of us. "I think I will write down that they turned on each other and killed one another in the confusion." He leaned down to Lena and said conspiratorially, "It will look better in the report that way. We don't want to confuse the other adults with too many details."

Lena nodded, then looked away.

I didn't know if Berger believed Lena, or if he merely believed she was a confused child. Either way, he was moving on. I wasn't going to dispute her version of events until we could sort out details later. After everything I had seen, I wasn't going to dismiss her out of hand. Something had killed the kidnappers, and my brief review of the crime scene told me that they hadn't turned on each other. Something else had killed all of them.

Berger pulled out a pen and pad. "While my men are taking statements, could you please tell me what you have pieced together about this trafficking organization?"

In twenty minutes, Pearson and I had done an awful lot while waiting for the police to show up.

Lena had been picked up in her orphanage in Poland. That's where thirty of the children had come from. The orphanage had been created in part by secular EU pressures and funded by the same forces behind said pressure—much to my surprise, it was Lord Fowler and Lady Toynbee. Apparently, Brexit hadn't come fast enough, and the British Atheists had been one of the key power players pushing a radically secular agenda, to such a point where the EU had thrown its weight into twisting Poland's arm to get rid of religious-run orphanages.

I had to explain that Toynbee and Fowler were connected to Jihadists in London before they had "disappeared." Which was true, they did disappear ... into a ball of fire.

The Fowlers and their Jihadi band of buggers might be dead, but apparently, their apparatus was still up and running. The British, secular face of the operation had allowed it to function without an issue since Poland was incredibly wary of Islam and anyone coming out of the Sandbox. The Fowler name and face on the operation had made it all too easy for the human trafficking to work.

After Lena had been taken, the next step was Adara's tour bus. Adara's family had decided to go on a vacation, getting away from it all, and thought that Adara could go on a school trip.

The tour guide offices were in Poland.

Kommissar Berger frowned. "Ah. That should be interesting."

"How so?"

"German inquiries into Poland?" he asked incredulously.

I simply nodded. "So there's very little you can do."

"Correct." He looked me right in the eye as he slid away his pen and pad. "*I* can do very little. I also cannot *prevent* anyone from their own investigations in other countries. Anything that might happen *in Poland* is purely Poland's problem. And it is no concern of mine. *Verstain?*"

I nodded. I understood clearly. "How about here?"

"Here?" Berger gave a very relaxed shrug. "This was clearly gang activity. A falling out amongst criminals. And you, a poor tourist, got caught in the crossfire."

I nearly objected to the blatant lie, but then I remembered that this was Europe. There was no legal transparency here. There wasn't even a right to free speech here. No freedom of the press. The story was whatever the governments allowed to be the story. Germany, in particular, didn't advertise crimes by Muslims because they didn't want to "upset" the Muslims. There were at least two massive movements by the German populace for a crackdown on criminal activity by refugees—the press labeled them as "far-Right movements," even when it was a movement populated with women raped by men who answered to the description of "Middle Eastern."

Berger's voice was thick with disgust and sarcasm when he said, "We wouldn't want visitors thinking that we had a rape problem among Muslim refugees. Would we?" He scoffed and shook his head.

Lena held to me with one hand, reached out and patted Berger on the arm, as though reassuring him.

Berger smiled gently at her. "And what about you two? Adara, would you like to go home?"

Adara nodded sleepily. She hadn't slept well for the better part of a day, and I was the safety blanket to end all safety blankets. "*Dedecek* wasn't home."

I nodded to confirm Adara's statement. "We tried calling her grandfather. He wasn't home, and the synagogue where he works didn't answer."

Berger raised a brow. "He works at a synagogue?"

Lena answered for Adara. "He's a rabbi."

I nodded. "Her parents are away for a while. She can't go home until someone answers."

Berger nodded slowly. "Perhaps you could do us a favor, then. If your travels *do* take you to Poland, you could technically drop Adara on the way. Especially if you drive."

I blinked. He had a point. I hadn't even considered it. Then again, I was more familiar with the twists and turns of New York than I was with Europe.

Both Adara and Lena hugged my arms tighter. "I think they approve of the idea of me taking them."

Berger smiled. "Can't imagine why."

I arched a brow. "Adara is Jewish, so she's allergic to Germans. Lena is Polish ... so *she's* allergic to Germans."

Berger's eyes narrowed. "Yes. I see."

Maybe my snark was a little too heavy for once. "Sorry."

PEARSON, THE TWO GIRLS, AND I ALL MADE IT TO THE sidewalk. We walked out the back way, around to the front.

Pearson held Adara's hand, I held Lena's, and they both held each other's. We would have looked very strange if anyone had been on the street. The car from the rectory swung around, and the four of us piled in.

"Did you kill the monster?" Adara asked.

I looked at the two girls. "Which monster?"

Lena looked up at me with her big blue eyes. "The woman with the cat eyes."

Jayden. "She got away."

"Are you going to kill the monster?"

I thought about the cache of guns in the trunk that Pearson and I had transplanted and smiled.

As I said, Pearson and I had done an awful lot of work while we were waiting for the cops.

"Yes, Lena," I told her. "We're going to kill the monster."

Pearson and I were put up in a rectory. The girls were taken by some German nuns so they could be cleaned up and dressed.

I changed into fresh sweatpants and an NYPD T-shirt. Pearson simply slipped off his jacket and hung it on a hook.

Pearson steepled his fingers and said, "So, did we withhold anything else from the authorities that we should discuss?"

"Talk to me about Asmodeus," I told him.

Pearson's eyes went up. "Asmodeus? He's a kind of demon. Antagonist in the Book of Tobit. His name is about wrath, though many associate him with lust."

I scoffed, mildly amused. "A demon of lust and rage. Sounds perfect for a rape gang."

The priest nodded. "Indeed. But why do you ask?"

I shrugged. "Jayden—the succubus? She said that they were going to raise her master. Her master is Asmodeus."

Pearson winced. "And she said 'raise'? Not 'summon'?"

"I believe so. Why? Did I miss a memo?"

Pearson frowned and even wrung his hands. "How did you like fighting a possessed serial killer?"

I winced at the memory. I almost felt the prison bars spear through my chest again. "I hated it, thanks. Why?"

"This was the low-key version. You said that XO referred to a manifested demon as a Cthulhu? Well, that's more or less what we're talking about. And the form Asmodeus took ... let's call it a dragon. It might be easier."

I flinched. A dragon was the easy part? What was the hard part going to look like? "What else?"

Pearson shrugged. "It depends on the lore and whom you wish to believe. There's a story about how he is the worst of demons. There are stories that make him seem like Loki. There are suggestions that he married Lilith—which is another conversation entirely. Though it is thought that she inspired myths about succubi."

I rolled my eyes. *Of course, it would.*

Pearson waved it away dismissively. "Bah. It wouldn't be the first time that occult BS has happened in Germany."

I nodded. "I know. I've seen the History Channel documentaries."

Pearson scoffed. "If you can call them that. But even before the Nazis, there were cults springing up all over the place. A lot of them were absorbed into the Nazi machine."

I frowned. Middle Eastern gunmen with demons and occult workings. Depending on how they worked them, it was going to get messy. And Bokor Baracus was sufficiently pissed off at them, because their check bounced. I didn't know if that was a metaphor or not.

"Don't we have any additional exorcists kicking around that we can call for backup?" I asked. "I'm going to guess that if one succubus can be a random minion walking around their haunts, it can't be the only one."

"I *am* your exorcist."

I rolled my eyes. "I mean in-country exorcists. German exorcists."

Pearson's eyes hardened. "I'm *it*. Western Europe doesn't believe in possession anymore. They don't believe in exorcism anymore. The United States has more exorcists, and you only have around half the number you need. There are 180 dioceses in the Colonies, and you should have one exorcist per diocese. You have somewhere between 75 or 100, they don't publish the number. It's why I'm your partner. You can't *get* anybody else. The rest of us are overworked."

I grimaced. "That's odd. I wonder how I got so many priests for Riker's Island. I had over a hundred priests show up."

Pearson sniffed and dismissed the question. "It was a prison riot and someone had a phone tree. I doubt most of those priests even said a prayer from the Rite. Hell, there are probably some who wouldn't even be able to quote a prayer from it that they didn't hear out of the *Exorcist* movie."

I flinched. "Great. We're screwed."

"Now, now. It's not that bad. A decade or two ago, there were hardly any. This has actually improved a great deal in recent years, with a push from the Vatican. We just need more, that's all. I think we have to have a long talk with the Bishops around the world. Preferably with a cricket bat. Maybe a hurling stick."

I sighed and slumped in the chair. "Great. On that positive, uplifting note, I'm going to bed."

Pearson nodded. "Good idea. I presume that we're driving to Poland tomorrow?"

"It's the only place I can think of to go next. Adara's entire busload of tourists were just taken off the road. That doesn't sound like something you do without advanced planning. Someone had timed it so that they could take the orphans from Poland, drive down through Czechoslovakia, hit the bus, and push on to Munich. That's a ton of luck or a perfectly executed plan. You don't have it unless you have the bus route, as well as insiders at the orphanage."

Pearson sighed. "About that, I called some friends in Poland."

"The answer is 'orphanage? What orphanage?' Right?"

"Not quite. There are records of an orphanage being there. And Lena was perfectly correct. The Fowlers were attached to it."

I waited for the other shoe to drop. "And...?"

"And, as of an hour ago, it was cleared out. No one is there. Nothing. A lot of ashes."

I rolled my eyes. "Of course. That's not important—not to us, anyway. How many people can XO reach out to? Because if the Fowlers did this across the EU, someone's going to need to stomp them into the dirt."

Pearson nodded sharply. "Already on it."

I sighed as I lurched out of the chair. "Still heading to Poland tomorrow. How long is the drive?"

"Nine hours. If we're lucky."

"Out of here at nine, there by six. With luck. Sounds like a plan." I fell face first on the bed.

As I closed my eyes, I thought about Lena's statement. Kill the monster. Before my life had become rife with demons and exorcists and magic, I wouldn't have entertained the idea of going in with the intent to kill a perp. I had even arrested as many of the death cult as would be taken alive. It took a visitation by an angel to make me consider that I should go out to smite evil.

But then, that's when everyone I fought was human. Now I had to wonder how human the humans were. No, I didn't think of them as inhuman because they were Muslim or even Jihadists—I meant that they were actively working with creatures from the depths of Hell, how much of their own humanity was left? How many had to sacrifice how much in order to get infernal reinforcements? Was there even the possibility of redemption left for them?

Normally, I would say that about anybody. But for all I knew, the first payment in the occult was the soul.

But no. The monster Lena wanted dead was "Jayden." And I was all for putting a stake through its heart. She had threatened children. She had Adara's tour leader raped to death (we had found her body. We didn't need to tell her—Lena had figured it out). And I had just come fresh from holding the little bundle of joy that was my Grace. You could be certain that I was going to put that infernal creature into the ground.

As I had to tell people often, when asking "What would Jesus do?" always remember that "Grabbing a whip and flipping tables" was always an option.

It was time to flip some tables.

I was completely asleep in a matter of seconds. I had no dreams. I had no visions. I had nothing but darkness.

I MADE IT TO MORNING MASS WITH LENA AND PEARSON. Adara had breakfast without us. It was served by an old nun who had learned how to cook Kosher from the previous Mother Superior. Let's just say it wasn't the first time this group of nuns had sheltered Jews in Germany.

During Mass, I offered to hold Lena's hand during the Our Father. She flinched at first, then forced herself to grab my hand and hold tight.

She expects to be hit when offered affection, I observed. *She's been beaten before. Note to self, see if the orphanage organizers can be thrown into the darkest hole Poland owns.*

We were on the road at nine in the morning, and Pearson drove. Our first stop was Prague.

Once we were safely on the highway and settled in for the

long haul, I turned in my seat and looked at Lena. "So, how long have you hurt people with your mind?" I asked.

Lena frowned and thought about it. "A few months." She shrank in the seat. "I don't do it on purpose. Until last night."

I waved it away. "Not my concern. I'm just asking for information. And in terms of last night, that was fine. But until you can control it better, I suggest you don't rely on it."

Lena blinked, and furrowed her brow. "What do you mean?"

"It's like a gun. If you don't know how to control it, you might hurt yourself, or make the situation worse. If you're in a situation where you're well hidden, trying to use your mind and *missing* might give away that you're in the room."

Pearson gave me a brief glance as he sped past a car. "Excuse me, but what exactly are we talking about?"

"Lena can hurt people with her mind," I said casually. "I'm thinking it's telekinesis. From what I saw in the garage last night, it's the only way to explain some of the angles of attack on the ones I didn't kill. Unless there was a giant, a midget, and a third man armed with a rope, a knife and a baseball bat."

Pearson said nothing for a moment. "Indeed? Well, that makes things interesting."

I nodded. "See. It's nothing that upsetting."

Pearson raised his voice and angled his head, trying to talk to Lena. "Quite. In fact, from the few cases of telekinesis we have recorded, you'd be about the right age for the onset."

Lena frowned. "Tele—"

"Telekinesis," I said, worried that it might be a gap in her vocabulary. "You can move things by thinking about it."

"Oh. Hussar? Could I have stopped them from hurting Adara's grownup?"

"No," I said plainly and clearly and immediately. "You'd need more practice with your aim. What I saw at the garage, you could have easily hurt her as the men who hurt her. You need more finesse. More..."

Pearson supplied, *"Precyzja."*

Lena nodded. "Oh."

Adara leaned forward. "Hussar? When are we going to see my *Dedecek?*"

"About four hours," I answered. "Assuming nothing goes wrong."

Three hours in, we called the number Adara gave me for her grandfather's synagogue, which had us redirect to the hospital. When her grandfather had been told that Adara's bus had gone missing, he had had a heart attack.

Rabbi Yedidiah Tiah Weil looked like every other Orthodox Rabbi, a face buried under a head of curls and a beard that could stuff a pillow. His hair had gone gray, and his deep, calm brown eyes were behind wire rims so faint they were barely there.

For a man who had just had a heart attack, he didn't look that bad. He was probably too pale, but he was sitting up, in bed, and reading a book.

He saw Adara and smiled broadly. This triggered off a five-minute discussion in Czech where I just loomed out in the hall-way, out of the way. Lena was next to me. She didn't want to let Adara out of her sight either.

According to ... everyone who translated for me, Adara's parents were big money. Her father was in construction all over the planet. It may have been part of the reason why Adara hadn't been molested in any way. They may have wanted her for ransom. Or they just wanted to make certain they had "unspoiled goods" for the "market"...

And yes, even *trying* to think like the sex traffickers made me ill.

Lena gripped my hand. "Hussar. What will happen to me?"

I kept my face impassive. I had considered that on the way through Prague. Adara had to come with me because we were delivering her to her grandfather. Lena had to come because Adara wouldn't leave her side. Unless the Rabbi left the hospital *this minute* (unlikely) or had friends to send her to, Adara would be sticking with us. This meant Lena was imperative. That put off the question of what to do with her until then. I didn't want to kick Lena to the curb, but I also wanted her out of the line of fire. Leaving her with the Polish orphanage system was out of the question, especially if Fowler had screwed it up half as badly as I thought he might have. Poland was still better than most of Eastern Europe, but not if it had been wrecked by policies forced on them by the EU.

It was just easier to tell her the truth. "I don't know. My immediate concern is making certain you don't get hurt while the monster is still out there."

Lena nodded solemnly and said nothing. She just squeezed my hand. It was strange for an orphan who had been in the system to be this used to physical contact. I'm sure someone would dismiss it as an attachment disorder, but I just chalked it up to being the one who rode in on the white horse.

Adara raced out of the hospital room. "*Dedecek* wants to talk with you, Komissar Nolan."

I nodded and walked with Lena and Adara into the hospital room. Rabbi Weil waved at me to come in. He pointed to Lena and Adara and spoke straight to them. Adara pointed at Lena. Lena nodded. The Rabbi looked right at me and spoke as though I knew his language.

Lena said, "He wants me to tell you that he wants to thank you for saving his granddaughter."

I gave a little bow in place of a nod. It was equal parts respecting my elders, being polite to a total stranger, and respecting a religious elder. "I was only doing my job."

Rabbi Weil gave a chuckle and spoke again. The last part he said straight to Lena.

Lena smiled. "When I was twelve, Americans freed me from a German camp. They said the same thing." She giggled. "It's an American thing, he says."

I shrugged. "Maybe."

The Rabbi spoke again, and laughed at the end. "He says 'My second son runs a construction company. Adara's older brothers are part of the company. They all went to San Francisco for a convention. Adara was to be away at camp. Adara seems attached to Lena. Lena seems attached to you. Could you take care of Adara for a day or two? Until they let me out of here? I normally wouldn't trust a strange' ... 'goy, but you saved her. We can probably trust you for a few minutes.' "

I nodded. "Of course."

" 'And, if you need anything at all, call me. My son is such a good' .... 'mensch'?" Lena paused. "He will give you anything he can."

I nodded politely and thanked him. I couldn't for the life of me imagine what his son would or could do, unless they had an army of demon-killing machines that I could borrow. *That would be so nice.*

Except I paused. Something occurred to me. I leaned in close to him and whispered one word. He paused, looked at Lena, then me, and then Rabbi Weil nodded.

I told Lena, "As many as possible." She translated.

He nodded, and we shook on it.

We said our goodbyes. I waited until we were in the parking lot before I asked the question preying on me since the conversation with Rabbi Weil started. Since Lena translated instead of his granddaughter, I had deduced that Rabbi Weil had asked Lena and Adara, who spoke better English. Adara had pointed to Lena.

Which meant the Polish orphan knew English better than the daughter of wealthy parents.

Which led to one question. "Lena, how did you learn English? Adara knows some, but she also grew up in a nicer household than mine and knows more languages than I do. But you speak better English."

Lena shrugged. "I listen when people think. It's easier when they think. I understand them, even when the words don't mean much."

Sure. Psychic child. Why not? No stranger than my usual Tuesday.

Lena giggled.

At six o'clock at night, I walked into the Polish tourist agency that had set up Adara and her tour bus. Adara and Lena were back with Pearson.

I opened the tourist agency door and forced myself not to react to the smell of sin.

Only one person was in the main office. She was tall and blonde, with high cheekbones, hourglass shape, long torso.

Do succubi come pressed out of a mold or something? Change facial features and hair color, and you're done?

At least, this made it easier for me to lie my way through my story. Lying to a succubus wouldn't bother my conscience. "Hello!" I chirped, trying for my best eager executive look. "I'm Tommy Pearson...I'm sorry, do you speak English?"

The succubus smiled at me without even the trace of impatience. She rose and walked over to me at the front desk. She slid her shapely tush on the desk. She leaned back on the desk with one arm and took my tie with the other. Her leg rubbed against my hip and slid her hand up and down.

All I could think was, *Do succubi have a fetish for neckwear?*

"Of course, Mister Pearson," she said.

I was not surprised that she made certain to keep just enough of an accent to sound exotic and sexier. She already had a base-level seduction up and running. It may not have been something she could turn off, based on her nature.

Either way, I had to let it effect me. If my encounter with Jayden was any indication, successfully resisting this succubus would tip her off to the setup. So I smiled and lied through my teeth.

"Hi, I'm in the entertainment business. In about three minutes, I'm going to have to ride herd on about fifty executives from out of town, and they need..." I deliberately paused for the salacious implications. *"Entertainment.* If you know what I mean." I leaned in conspiratorially towards her, putting me over her lap and putting my face within inches of hers. "Do you know what I mean? I don't want the language barrier to mess this up."

She smiled so seductively, so automatically, she must have rehearsed it. Her eyes flared. "I know exactly what you mean, Mister Pearson."

As her bright blue eyes flared, so did her power.

My body reacted as predictably as one would expect. Unlike before, it didn't hit me as hard as it should have. Her artifice was showing, and it was a turn-off.

I looked deep into her eyes and superimposed Mariel's face over hers. I suddenly had the impulse to grab her and make love to her on the desk right then and there.

The succubus in front of me blinked and cocked her head to one side. She was confused at the effect. It wasn't the lust she was used to invoking. She sensed marital fidelity and passionate love and had no idea how to process it.

She tamped down on her power and pushed me lightly away with her fingertips. "If you want, I can show you some of the ... *services* we provide."

I smiled at her naturally. She thought I was lascivious and

ready to get in her pants. I just really wanted to find out where she lived so I could raid her offices when they were closed, then raid her home when she was at work.

"We?" I asked with my smile in place.

Her smile seemed ... hungry. "My three roommates and I all work here."

I checked her desk. Her name was just "Nikki." I looked back at her. "I would love to meet them, Miss Nikki...?"

"Nowak," she answered.

Nowak was a last name so common, it was more or less the Poland version of "Smith."

Nikki waved me onward with a finger. She was very confident in her ability to pick up a man with a wink and a smile. I was happy to let her think that.

"What about my rental car?" I asked.

"We are just down the block."

Of course you are. "Perfect."

I walked into the apartment building and followed Nikki's butt up the staircase. She expected me to look, and I met her half-way. I superimposed my wife on her form and figure, even her walk. Nikki paused the moment I did this, but only for a second. She proceeded to walk up to the top floor.

She had a penthouse.

Of course, she did.

Nikki opened the door and turned around to grab me by my tie. She yanked on it hard.

The tie came right off. She was confused that it was a clip on.

I smiled sheepishly. "I never learned how to tie a tie," I lied. It was a standard police tie, so perps *couldn't* do what she just tried to do.

Nikki shrugged, tossed it over her shoulder, and grabbed me by my lapels. She kissed me deeply, flaring her power.

My blood burned, my heart rate shot up, and the erection I'd had for the last fifteen minutes became painful.

Nikki pressed me up against the wall and held me at arm's length. "Girls!" she called out in a singsong voice. "I brought dinner!"

"Hussar," I said clearly and distinctly.

Nikki ignored me. She turned away towards the rest of the penthouse suite, thinking she had left me in a daze. "But don't finish him. He's going to be bringing more chum in a few months."

I fell behind her in step. She may not have expected that but didn't think I was a threat.

Her three "roommates" came out to play. They were all in various states of undress.

One of them locked eyes on me and pointed. "That's him! That's the man from Munich!"

It was Jayden. Her skin and hair had grown back so it looked like she had never been burned by holy water. But her eyes, and fingers, ignited with Hellfire, ready to turn me to charcoal.

If you've ever seen a Mass card, or a saint card, they tend to be palm-sized, solidly laminated pieces of paper. They are blessed and consecrated. They're also incredibly sturdy.

They're also handy in fighting off demons.

In that long, long flight from London to Rome a few months back, during a conversation about weaponizing holy objects in the battle against evil, Mass cards were a particularly difficult thing to use. They weren't aerodynamic unless one was a practiced magician.

However, taping a razor blade to the edge of a holy card meant that one got penetration.

I didn't wait for Nikki to react. I grabbed her by the shoulder with my left hand and reached around her throat with my right.

Then I slit her throat with a holy card, digging deep into the meat and muscles and veins of her neck. Between the razor penetrating the skin, and the holy card burning and sizzling, melting away the fake skin manifested for the "Nikki" form, I cut her throat straight to the bone. I drew her a new smile from behind one collarbone all way to another. Then I thrust forward across the back of her neck, severing it at the other end.

Nikki reached forward for her "roommates," and made a gurgling sound as she took one step.

Then her head fell off. Both it and her body hit the floor and melted away.

I leaped to one side as Jayden threw fireballs at me, trying to cook me. She set a closet on fire.

One of her other succubi grabbed her hand and shoved it down. "Don't destroy the apartment. You'll get us too much attention. There are four of us and one of him. Doesn't matter how powerful he is."

I came back up to my feet and stood out in front of the fiery closet. "You think you can take me? Come and get it."

Jayden and her sidekicks spread out, Jayden in the middle. One had taken the shape of a Japanese woman, the other was black. Between the four of them, they could cover many of the preferences of the men on the planet. Probably also the women who were into that sort of thing. The black succubus was on my right, on the same wall as the door. The Japanese was on my left, near the couch.

So I attacked.

I leaped for the Japanese. I wanted the cover of the couch, and I wanted to be as far away from the door as possible. As I jumped for her, I grabbed the pistol from the small of my back and chopped down with it, hitting her on the side of the head with the pistol grip. Her head snapped to one side. I jammed the muzzle under her chin and pulled the trigger.

The bullet impact drove her head straight back. She fell back onto the couch. I whirled to the other two and sidestepped away from Jayden as I shot her and her black succubus friend. The bullet strikes made them lose a step. I made it around the couch and swung back to the Japanese and shot her once in the face.

Every bullet I fired in that apartment had hit the mark.

None of the bullet strikes had even scratched the skin.

I reached into my pocket as the succubus on the couch stood up. She shook her head as though she were dazed, then looked at me, pissed off and hungry.

I threw the holy salt from my pocket into her face, then sent six rounds to join it. This time, the bullets penetrated. The holy salt burned and softened her up for the bullets. The bullets punched into her face, driving grains of holy salt into her. She screamed and grabbed her face like the Wicked Witch of the West.

The black succubus leaped for me, going for my face with her claws. I blocked it with my left arm. I jammed the gun under her chin and pulled the trigger. It was like I had punched her a little.

Then I smacked her with my left hand, covered in holy salts. She roared, grabbed me, and hurled me over to Jayden.

Jayden grabbed me by the neck with one hand and smacked away my gun with the other. She then slipped both arms around mine and clasped her hands together at the small of my back.

"This is more like it," Jayden said.

The black succubus darted in front of me. Her sharp teeth were showing. "We'd have fun with you, but I'm too hungry to wait."

Then the door kicked in, and the flash bangs went off. The succubi must have had perfect hearing, because the black one grabbed her ears, screaming in pain. The tactical team charged in and opened fire. Three of them had high-pressure water packs on their backs, the type firemen had with fire suppressants. They sprayed down the black succubus like she was on fire. She held up her hands and unleashed an unholy wail as her flesh melted away under the heavy spray of holy water.

I couldn't break Jayden's grip but was taller than her. I leaned forward sharply and turned around, presenting her back to the spray from the tactical team. Jayden was fast, though. Before I could turn fully, she broke her grip and shoved off me. I was sent flying against the wall; she went flying out the window.

On the way from Prague to Poland, Father Pearson had spent some time on the phone. He had started making calls ever since we stopped at the hospital. He was able to do this because Poland was special. Western Europe may not have believed in demons or the need for exorcists; it may have also decided to ignore any and all threats that involved Islam.

Poland, however, believed in demons. They had lived with demonic Nazis and Demonic Communists. Poles also believed that Muslims could be a threat, and that, in both cases, they should be stepped on as hard and as often as possible.

So when Pearson told his Polish police contacts that there was a Muslim sex trafficking ring smuggling out little Polish orphans, the Poles were pissed off and ready to break in some doors.

When Pearson also explained that there were demonic forces involved, the Poles were only a little skeptical. But they had no problem kicking in the door and melting two naked women into puddles of goo just by spraying them with holy water.

How did they know to kick in the door? Or that they were facing succubi?

Because I was wearing a listening device, and my stress word was "Hussar."

One of the commandos helped me to my feet, then clapped me on the back.

Another one grabbed me by the shoulders and lead me to the door. He pointed at the stairs and looked at me quizzically. I translated it as *Do you need help going down the stairs?*

I nodded and waved him off. *I can make it.*

He nodded, slapped me on the back, and I dragged myself down several flights of stairs. Because an old European building didn't have elevators. Eh. I would live.

I felt strangely exhausted on my way down the stairs. I didn't think that the combat would have done that much to me. I had been beaten worse, and harder, by bigger bad guys.

Let's see, you went from a twelve-hour plane ride, into a night-club fight, slept a few hours before being stuck in the car for most of a day, then got thrown around by demonic prostitutes after being pumped full of whatever they use for seduction. No. No reason to be tired.

I stepped outside the apartment. Pearson and the girls would be back near the mobile command center. Lena had no problem being surrounded by fellow Poles. Adara was fine as long as she was with Lena. And Pearson got along well with everybody.

But I just had to rest for a moment. I sat down on a bench outside the apartment building and closed my eyes.

The bench creaked as someone sat next to me. I opened my eyes and looked over. It was a big, strapping young man, maybe in his mid-20s, with clear crystal blue eyes and neatly combed black hair. He looked like a classical movie star. A Polish Rhett Butler.

He was also dressed in solid white. I felt like I should know him.

I gave him a little wave and forced myself to relax.

"Detective Nolan," he said, in a rich, deep voice, tinged with a Polish accent.

I did a double take at him. "Have we met?" I asked.

He smiled. He fingered the gold cross at his chest. "I know you. You may recall who I am."

I looked him up and down, a tingle went down my spine. "So, you're John Paul II?"

He smiled and gave a little wave. "Hi."

I took a deep breath, held it, and let it out slowly. "Okay. Great. What can I do for you?"

He grinned. "I was sent to tell you to be not afraid."

I arched a brow. "Really? That's it?"

"Considering all you have to face? All you have faced?"

I frowned and shrugged. "Point taken. But don't you have better things to do? I'm relatively certain I have a guardian angel who could have done the courier work."

Pope Saint John Paul II grinned broadly. "Are you complaining about the messenger or the message?"

"Neither, really. Just curious." I sat back in the bench and let out a deep breath. "I'll tell you that these things do scare me."

The late Pope shrugged at me. "You have done well so far. What are you concerned about? That God will abandon you? Or that you will let everyone else down?"

I gave him a glare. "The latter, obviously. Everything I can do is predicated on my virtue. Which isn't something I gave a lot of thought to before this happened. I'm not sure it was ever challenged before."

He shook his head at me, his smile amused. "Come now. How often have you been tempted to strike someone who desperately deserved it and refrained? Even when you could get away with it?"

"Doesn't count," I told him. "How many hundreds of thousands of cops go through the same thing?"

"That is not my point. My point is you have often been tempted. And you have faced this temptation routinely. But you refrain from sinning. You protect your family. You protect strangers. You bring them into your house, into your life. You have adopted many simply because they had nowhere else to go."

"You're starting to sound like my wife."

"She has a point. There is a reason smarter ancient cultures saw the woman as the spiritual half to a man. When even the pagans can figure it out..." He shook his head. "I would not worry about the temptations you've faced. They will only get much, much worse from here."

Saint John Paul the Great patted me on the shoulder in the same "bro" clap that the Polish tactical guys did. "It is good to be wary. But be careful not to fall into the trap of obsessing over it. You're too busy for such things. Now, two things."

"Yes?"

"Call your wife. And *put on the ring.*"

I blinked, and he was gone.

I looked around. I half expected to wake up. I didn't. I was already awake.

I reached into my pocket and grabbed the Soul Ring. I was still wary of it. It was a power beyond reckoning. The full-sized rock could level a city. What could this do? And was I willing to find out?

I slipped the ring on my right ring finger.

The next time I confronted Jayden would be the last time. Hopefully, it wouldn't be because I hesitated to use everything at my disposal.

I called Mariel.

"Congratulations," she said when she picked up. "You waited a whole what? Two days without calling me! Eventually, we'll get you to go a week when you're busy getting shot at."

"Don't press your luck," I told her.

"Aren't you cute?"

"You sound mighty chipper for someone who endured labor not that long ago."

"Why not?" she asked me. "I have this perfect bundle of joy right here, and she's so perfect and cute and rrrrrrr."

It took me a moment to realize that our connection hadn't broken up. That was Mariel making growling noises. "Good. So no problems?"

"Of course not. Jeremy is being such a good boy and helping out. And how many supplies did you buy last week? I won't need to shop for at least the rest of the month, especially with you away. And if you're back before then, I don't have to worry about that, will I? And Father Freeman has talked about flying down for a little. So if I need anything done, I can twist his arm."

I rolled my eyes. "Yeah. I'm sure you'll need to do that."

"Tell me what's been happening?"

I did. It took a while. She only gave the occasional comment here and there.

On Jayden: "Be sure to slap that bitch for me."

"I'll be sure to do that when I can."

On Lena: "She sounds so sweet."

She didn't comment again until, "JP-Two? Really? What did he say?"

I told her. She said, "We know what that means, don't we?"

I nodded to myself. "Probably. We should talk about it a little later, though."

"Absolutely. What else was there?"

I told her.

I rose and walked back to where we left the mobile command post. Pearson, Lena, and, Adara were outside. Pearson was a few yards away, talking to one of the commandos.

He speaks Polish, too?

Lena, meanwhile, sat with Adara on a bench. Adara was curled up next to her, with Lena stroking her hair like Adara was a pet. Her cute little features were scrunched up in thought. I walked up to her without her eyes tracking me.

"You look very thoughtful," I told her quietly, trying not to wake Adara. I should have known better since children seemed to go from "run" to "dead asleep" in a matter of seconds.

Lena started a little, looking at me. Very seriously, she said, "I'm thinking about where I go after this is over."

I like how she sounds like she's contemplating a move. "Well, let's start with something simple," I said casually. "What do you like to do?"

"Read." She smiled brightly. "Have you ever read Henryk Sienkiewicz? Or perhaps *Wiedzmin*? The... um ... Witcher?"

"I've heard of them. I've never had a chance to read much fiction, though."

Lena nodded seriously. "I hope to finish them one day. They're long. I haven't been able to be in one place long enough to finish anything but short stories." Her eyes caught a glint off of the Soul Ring. She reached over and grabbed my hand. I let her pull it close. "Crusader?"

She had recognized the cross. "After a fashion."

Lena smiled. "Good. Keep it simple. The flag of the Holy League is too complicated. You chose well."

I shrugged. "I didn't pick it. It's sort of a gift from the Vatican."

Lena's eyes went wide. "You know the Pope! Wow!"

"Not quite, just some of the bureaucratic functionaries. They know some jewelers. It's a bit of a souvenir."

Lena nodded solemnly. "It's good. You should have a standard."

I smiled a little. "I'm a cop. Technically, I have a flag. And emblems."

Lena shook her head. "No. A knight needs a standard. You're going to kill the barbarians at the gate. But you just need a horse and a sword to be a true Hussar. Better to kill them with."

My eyebrows went up a little, but not by much. "I'd say you're a little bloodthirsty for your age, but my son is twelve."

Lena's eyes narrowed. "Monsters need to be killed. You must slay dragons."

I paused for only a moment. I was used to conversations like this with Jeremy. "I'm going to have to work on my aim. A dragon is too well-armored to penetrate anything but the eye."

Pearson, with his characteristically good timing, wandered over from the police. "Good news. We have a lead among Jayden's papers. It's an address in Berlin."

I didn't have to look at my watch to know we'd have to drive through the night to get anywhere. "Should we talk to the Germans?"

"The locals are on it," Pearson said. "As Lena so properly observed earlier, the Poles and Germans are not very happy with each other. But the Politzei couldn't ignore information from another country."

I considered Kommissar Berger's look of disgust with the German authorities. "Don't be too certain."

Pearson shrugged. "It's an address on the outskirts of Berlin. *Blankenburger Pflasterweg* 97, Berlin 1 3 1 29."

"Where is it?"

"Morderburg."

"Murderberg?" I asked Pearson.

The priest sighed and started again.

It was called Mörderberg.

"What is that?" I asked again. "A suburb or Mordor?"

Mörderberg was "Murderers' Mountain. "It was really a series of dark, soulless buildings built in the "plattenbau" style of communist public housing in East Germany. They were literal slabs of concrete slapped together and called a building.

Or in this case, a prison.

The *Volkspolizeikaserne Blankenburg*, or the Barracks for the riot police, was about as grim as anything you can imagine under communism. Having all of the windows bashed in just added to the atmosphere of "slasher film." Add rubbish strewn across the concrete didn't help matters. I had been to decommissioned airfields with more character.

This used to be a barracks for East Germany's dreaded Volk-spolizei-Bereitschaft (VPB), the "Standby People's Police," para-military riot police, part of the armed forces, answerable to the GDR's Interior Ministry. To keep the local populace in check.

The Stasi, the East German people's police, were considered a subtle scalpel. The VPB was the jackhammer.

The Blankenburg barracks was home to the riot police's 10th Company, and they were only part of the fun. The layout included a weapons workshop and a supply depot. On the other side of the high barbed wire secured fence was a dorm for engineering students ... I wondered if they had wanted to become engineers, or if it was part of their sentence.

Even the grassy parts around the barracks looked look desolate. I had seen photos of Dartmoor, England, that looked brighter and more cheerful. Here, it looked like a cross between the Great Grimpen Mire and Mordor. The parts of New Zealand used for Mordor looked more lively. I expected the Hound of the Baskervilles to pop out and howl any minute.

The five acres of concrete and misery had been earmarked by the Stasi to become a "detention center for foreign enemies of the state and individuals the state deemed suspicious." But they had never gotten around to using it. I couldn't imagine that they were in a rush. No one else wanted it because of the asbestos used in the construction.

Over the years, arsonists and other vandals had taken the time to test their skills on the twenty or so buildings. They were made of concrete, so unless the arsonists brought a demolition team, the buildings weren't going anywhere.

It only took us six hours to drive there from Krakow. Yes, *only*. It would take me that long to drive from New York City to upstate New York, to heck with another country.

Our timing on Morderberg had an additional creepy factor that we should have accounted for. Not only was it after midnight when we arrived, but Morderberg's barracks were hidden behind a layer of trees, on a one-lane road (in each direction) with no streetlamps.

My first and only thought was *Can we come back here in daylight? Please?*

But I had been the one to argue for going immediately. Jayden had escaped, and she had wings. I couldn't begin to guess at her airspeed, but it had to be faster than we could drive. She likely went to warn her people. With luck, they wouldn't have evacuated Morderberg already.

The German *Politzei* had called after two hours. Some uniforms had done a drive-by, and they hadn't seen anything.

An hour after that, the *politzei* called us back and told us that the officers who drove past Morderberg had both disappeared. Either they had been too mesmerized by supernatural forces to call into the station house, or whatever was out there had stayed well hidden until the cops had checked in, then eaten them.

More likely the cops were mesmerized. If they had done the drive-by, whatever was hiding there would have no need to ambush them—it would just let them drive off. Unless they were really hungry.

We both told the *politzei* that they should *not* send people in after their men. But if they could tell the local cops not to crash our party, we would see if we could find their missing officers.

We just didn't tell them if their officers would be alive or dead when we found them.

When I told Lena and Adara that we would drop them off on our way, Lena didn't want me out of her sight. I told her that the last thing anyone needs is for them to be kidnapped by sex traffickers again.

"It's not like I can be two places at once."

"Yes you can," she answered.

How did she know that? I wondered. "As I tell my son, I try not to test the Lord my God. I recommend you do the same."

But she was right about one thing—stopping off at Munich

would take too long, and Pearson couldn't get a hold of anyone in Berlin.

So Adara and Lena would be coming with us, whether we liked it or not.

The darkness of the area was eerie. Except for certain sections of New Jersey highway, I was used to brightly-lit streets. Now, if the headlights didn't illuminate it, the night was a never-ending void. The dark usually didn't make me nervous, but that was before the dark had tried to eat me.

The worst part was that I couldn't see anything.

"Drive past," I told Pearson. "We'll find a place to park the car and the girls."

Less than a half-mile past Morderberg was a golf resort. It was perfect for our purposes. We called in and asked that the local cops didn't come to tow our car away. If they wanted to baby sit it, we wouldn't argue. We sent them our photos via text so that they could stay out of the way and not shoot us when we were cleaning up their mess.

Pearson pulled us into the golf course. We were quiet when we got out, closed and locked the door, leaving Lena and Adara curled up in the back seat together, asleep. We were also especially careful when we opened the trunk.

That's where we had all of the guns stolen from the Munich nightclub. Automatic rifles, pump-action shotguns, and a few paintball guns and ammo the Polish commandos had thrown into our truck—apparently, you could make splat balls out of holy water. Who knew?

Pearson took out some holy water, sprinkled it on the weapons as he said, "May the blessing of almighty God, Father, Son, and Holy Ghost, descend upon these weapons and upon whomever wears them in the defense of justice. Almighty God, in whose hand full victory rests and who also gave David miraculous strength to battle the rebellious Goliath: humbly we pray your mercy to bless these weapons by your life-giving mercy; and grant your servants who will to bear them, that they may use them freely and victoriously for strengthening and defending the widows, the orphans, and Holy Mother Church. Your mystical Body, against the attacks of all enemies visible and invisible. Through Christ our Lord."

"Amen," I added, then grabbed a collection.

"I bring not peace but the sword," Pearson muttered, "and my handy submachine gun."

I ended up with four guns—a rifle, a paintball gun, a shotgun, and a sidearm. The sidearm was at the small of my back, but the shotgun hung off my back, and the paintball gun dangled off of my shoulder like a Christmas tree ornament.

As we made our way alongside the one-lane road to Morderberg, I felt the night get colder as we got closer and closer to the grounds. I could feel that Very Bad Things had happened here. Even without my charisms, the dark itself felt oppressive. There was no moon, and the stars gave off nowhere near enough light to see by. The ground was uneven, and both of us had to pick through the landscape slowly and carefully. Pearson seemed to handle it a little better than I did, but not by much. For once, I wished night vision was a charism.

My own experience gave the night a little extra menace. I half expected the dark to come alive again so I could fight it. But there were no shadows to fight this time, and the only Soul Stone was on my finger.

We reached the complex and were met with a chain link fence and broken barbed wire. The fence was augmented near the corner of the facility with a sheet metal barrier. We easily hopped over that and slipped into Morderberg.

It was one step away from being a concentration camp—only there was more concrete all around. I would say it was special— but this was fairly typical for Soviet construction. Every three buildings formed a U. The blank gray concrete buildings had all their doors and windows smashed in. There was half-finished graffiti every so often.

Even the graffiti people couldn't be bothered coming back here.

It was a perfect place for a sex trafficking way station. The area was desolate, foreboding and well hidden. If you didn't know it was there already, you couldn't find it unless you were lucky. If you found it, it was uninviting. The only people who might want to go there visited haunted houses for fun ... and might not be missed if the visitors were disappeared.

The surrounding landscape looked like someone had already sown the ground with salt as far as the eye could see. It was flat, with patchy, lopsided growths of sickly grass and weeds. Inside the camp ground was wild, untamed growth ... to a point. The trees were barren and lifeless. The grass was two feet high, brown and dead. Bird's nests were empty, with tiny fragments of abandoned eggshells left behind. Nothing had nested here in ages.

Everything here was dead.

HP Lovecraft would have loved this place.

There were also two dozen buildings. Unless we got a sign, there would be an endless search.

Then I caught a whiff of evil on the air.

I put up a fist, signaling Pearson to stop. I tapped my nose to signal him what I picked up.

We walked along the concrete path, staying off of the dirt. I didn't think a concrete slab could hide a Bouncing Betty landmine.

We slipped along the wall of the second building. I didn't want to tip off a scout. The first U of buildings had the weathered and broken concrete courtyard facing away from the street. We moved as quietly as we could. We made it to the third building—which was the start of the second courtyard. That courtyard gave off a smell, so we approached cautiously.

I got to the corner of the building and looked out into the next courtyard, which was uneven dirt and haphazard growth and death.

In the center of the courtyard was a *politzei* cruiser. The lights were smashed out. The windows smashed in. Two police officers were dead on the ground with their throats torn out.

I pulled back, lest I be spotted, and thought over what the next move should be. My training told me to call for backup. From who? The *politzei* would probably be useless around here. From what I had seen on the Google map satellite images, the area could be cut off without inconveniencing any of the civilians. But it would require a solid ring of police—not only cutting off the roads but the endless desolate plains around the complex. It could be managed, but it would take time and military gear. But it would also require men with flexible minds. Jayden could have easily beaten us, warned everyone, and worse, hung around, or called in support from other supernatural creatures. I had fought off four succubi already—what if they had dozens more in way stations like this? The cops would have to be briefed, properly armed, and ready to go to war with the Devil.

And we're in a country where not even the bishops could be bothered getting exorcists.

This all assumed that the creatures holding slaves here didn't consider the hostages expendable, kill them all, and fly away, over the barricade.

These bad guys needed to be taken stealthily, until they were within arm's reach, then hit hard and fast by people who had an idea of what they were confronting.

It would have to be the two of us.

I sneaked a peek around the corner again. The building across the courtyard was as dark as any other in the complex. A quick scan showed me that one of these things was not like the other—one of them had movement. It was a long figure, hiding in the shadows. Meaning there was at least one scout. Depending on what type of creature the scout was, there might have been more of them, or they only needed one.

I pulled back and away from the corner. I didn't want either of us to be seen. However, we also needed to get to the scout. We were on the narrow end of the building, and it had only three windows on that side—one per floor. I slipped under the window and cupped my hands. Pearson took the hint, put one foot in my hands, and I pushed him up for the window. He grabbed it, hauled himself in, and aided me through the window when I leaped for it.

We had entered the urban district of Hell. Unfinished walls and ceilings, broken tiled floors, exposed pipes, and hanging wires. The halls were so narrow, Jeremy had wider closets. Shattered glass, dirty floors, rats that merely stared at us like we weren't an impressive threat, and cockroaches that clung to the ceiling, lest the rats eat them.

Lord, your work always takes me to the nicest places, I thought sarcastically.

Pearson tapped me on the shoulder and pointed to the rats and the roaches again. The rats weren't staring, and the roaches weren't hiding in fear. They were all dead. I couldn't smell their decay for the other smells of this home of horrors. Other bugs hadn't even dared to feast on the corpses.

Even the vermin died here.

Our path took us to the roof—the roof access door had been removed ages ago. We quietly crept along the metal roof. The scout in the building opposite us watched the ground, scanning between the main path, and the spaces in between the buildings.

He didn't look up.

We made it to the edge of the roof nearest the next building over. It was not a long jump, but it was a long way down in the dark.

We both made it across without an issue. We crept along the roof, then made another jump to the next building over.

I took a deep sniff as we crept along. The shape I had seen was on the third floor. The smell peaked and then dwindled. I took a step back, I'd found him. *Gotcha.*

One of the other things the Polish commandos had left us with was rope. Lots of rope.

I had Pearson hold one end, and tie it down to a piece of roof, measured out the distance to reach a window one floor below me.

Dear God, I really hope this is as accurate as I think it is. Because I need it to be pinpoint this time.

I took a hold on the rope, took a deep breath, and charged.

I ran to the edge of the roof and jumped off of it.

For a long moment, it felt like I hung in the air until the rope grew taut, and gravity snatched me back.

I swung down in an arc, right for the window.

From what I saw of the scout's face, he seemed very surprised when I crashed through the window, slamming into him with the soles of both boots. I knocked him back and landed on my feet.

He rolled to his feet and hissed at me. He lunged for me, and I grabbed his wrists.

His skin sizzled and smoked. He blinked, taken aback.

I took a moment, reared back, and head-butted him.

His head dissolved at the collision. His body turned to dust along with it.

I knew what it was because something similar had happened once before, in New Jersey, before they learned that I could take them.

This part of the sex trafficking network were vampires.

I helped Pearson come down and explained what happened with the scout.

"I at least understand why they only used one guy on patrol," I concluded. "But if it was a vampire, you'd think he'd have heard us coming."

Pearson shrugged. "In my profession, I have a combat prayer meditation state. It masks my presence to the supernaturally-enhanced senses of creatures like him. As long as I didn't make too much noise, he didn't sense me. You're probably like that naturally."

"Yay me. What about the effectiveness of the guns?"

Pearson shrugged. "It'll hurt them, but it won't kill them. That requires the usual."

"Let's go."

We make our way through the building, clearing floor by floor, only finding more rats and cockroaches. I could barely smell the evil over the scent of vermin.

Things were made easier for us when we got to the second floor and could just follow the screams.

Then we made it to the walkway over the lobby, and things got weird.

Even for me.

In the main lobby, it was standard in terms of big spaces meant to impress—a three-story main lobby. It had a level of walkway overhead that looked down into the space. I could only figure that it had several alternate uses at one point or another—prisoner processing, or indoctrination of new recruits.

The banner that hung from the railing? A giant red flag with a white circle in the center for the immense black Swastika.

In the main lobby, row upon row of black and silver-suited vampires with huge fangs. They were lined up in near, almost perfect rows, hands at their sides, heels together. Instead of the matching SS hat, it was a fez with the Swastika emblazoned on it.

What had been the desk for the front lobby had been moved back, up to a stage in front of the flag. On the desk was tied a naked woman. There was another vampire in a black and silver SS uniform standing over her with a ceremony knife, chanting something in a mix of Arabic and German.

Well, I thought. *This is different.*

The woman screamed again as she thrashed against the ropes. The man with the knife said something interesting, and the audience snapped to salute and cried, "Sieg Heil!"

He grabbed the hilt of the knife.

"Not. Gonna. Happen."

I grabbed the rail and swung myself over. I dropped the rifle so it dangled over my shoulder. I pulled out the combat knife I'd carried since I took it at the nightclub, stabbed the Nazi flag, and let gravity pull me down. The sturdy canvas flag kept me from accelerating too quickly. When I was ten feet over the floor, the leader with the ceremonial knife raised it above his head.

I pushed off of the flag, knife in hand, and dropped on the

leader, stomping him to the ground. I drove my fist through his face, making him disintegrate.

I came up with the knife and slashed at the woman's bindings. I grabbed her around the waist with my free hand and dragged her behind the metal desk. I dropped the knife, grabbed the AK, set it to fully automatic, then popped up again and roared as I unloaded the magazine into them like it was an old-school Tommy gun, and I was executing a drive-by shooting. They were clustered together in a tight formation, taking fire from consecrated bullets.

Pearson also fired from his position on the walkway above.

The Nazi Muslim vampires fell back... into formation. The front rank knelt, and the next two remained standing. They bared their fangs and their claws and opened fire with their own weapons.

They shot lightning from their fingers.

I retreated behind the desk. The metal sparked and crackled with electricity. Above me, Pearson ducked behind the banner and ran for it as the lightning set it on fire.

Nazi Muslim vampires who throw lightning. I guess this is my life now.

I quickly thought over the situation. There was no cover between the desk and the vampires. There would be no cover for me except for cover fire—assuming Pearson was on the ball. In a few seconds, the vampires might consider that they should stop relying on whatever supernatural lightning they were using and just beat me to death with a chair. Even if they spread out, we could waste time shooting individual vampires until we needed to change magazines—with their vampire speed, they could then close with me, disarm me, and force-feed me my own gun.

I need to close with them first so they don't grow a brain.

I poked the gun out over the desk and emptied the magazine into the ranks of vampires.

I ducked back, reloaded, then looked to the girl. She was curled up in a ball, her butt on the floor. I offered her the AK.

"Verstaten ... gun?" I asked, hoping to be understood.

"I *verstain* English better, but I can point and click," she said in a London cockney accent.

I restrained my shock and curiosity and thrust the rifle into her hands. I dropped two magazines on the floor in the hope that she could figure it out. I pointed to the left corner of the desk and said, "Count to five."

She set up position on the left as I made it to the right corner, unslinging the shotgun. It was a Mossberg 590 pump action with a 20-shot box magazine. I had loaded it with the "alternating special rounds" the Poles had thrown into the trunk.

She opened fire, then I charged out, blasting away with the shotgun.

The vampires' attention was split for barely a second, but that was enough for the first vampire to take a shotgun blast to the face with a consecrated shotgun round.

The next vampire saw me and threw lightning at me. I fired again. The ball of lightning was met with a blast of holy salt, dissolving the lightning bolt and then the vampire's face. He fell back with a scream.

I racked the shotgun again and fired.

What came out was a small blanket of fire that roared out into the cluster of vampires. The incendiary round burned over 4,000 degrees hot, with a heavy mix of magnesium. It didn't blanket the group, but it set six of them on fire—three who were kneeling were caught in the face. The ones standing had their uniforms set on fire. They leaped back, setting other members of the group on fire. All of them were in chaos.

They were called Dragon's Breath shells.

The Poles did not disappoint.

The vampires turned their attention to me and took fire from above and the side as the girl, and Father Pearson blasted into them on full auto—with the AK and his paintball gun. Several of the vampires turned to dust when the blessed bullets struck them in the head or the heart, burning away enough of either to kill them.

I charged into the cluster, racking the shotgun again and cut through them as the ammunition type alternated with each rack of the slide.

Ch-ch. Boom. Consecrated buckshot.

Ch-ch. Boom. Holy salt.

Ch-ch. Boom. Dragon's breath.

I was only feet away from them as I ran out of ammo. The girl and Pearson had stopped firing, worried that they might hit me.

I dropped the shotgun, swung around my paintball gun, and shot at them from point-blank range. One lunged for me, forgetting what happened to their leader. I backhanded his face away, and he disintegrated. Another one just got his hands to spark with lightning when I put five holy water splat balls into his mouth. It worked like acid as his mouth and neck dissolved away, effectively decapitating him.

I plowed into them, swinging with fists. The vampires had no concept of "retreat," so when I leaped on them, they basically dissolved into a pile of black uniforms.

I rolled onto my back, looking around frantically for more vampires.

Nothing.

I let out a breath of relief and let myself relax. *There was no way that should have worked. None. Thank you, God. I presume you made them stupid on purpose.*

The girl ran up to me. She was a brunette, I just noticed, with long brown hair that hadn't been cleaned in about a month or two. "Detective Nolan. You okay?"

I blinked. "Have we met?"

She smiled. "Guess you don't know me without clothes on. I'm Jillian. We met in London. You saved me from some kidnappers. My mate and I got you to the church after the riots. Looks like you saved me again."

I blinked, confused. I vaguely remembered Jillian from the London excursion. I was busy at the time being shot at. But I had saved her, and she made my life a heck of a lot easier after I had nearly been blown up in Toynbee Tower. "It looks like I didn't do a good job of saving your the first time if they went after you again."

Jillian shrugged. "They got me only a few days ago while I was going to a public loo. So I haven't had to put up with ... much. Not as much as some of the others I ran in to."

I winced. "I can imagine. Though I'm surprised. I'd have thought Kozbar's people would be staying low after Kozbar bought it."

Jillian frowned. "Kozbar's dead?" She waved at the piles of ash-covered SS uniforms and bullet-ridden fezes. "Someone should have told this lot. They kept talking like he was alive."

I winced. The last time I had seen Imam Kozbar, the Jihadi schmuck of the Whitechapel mosque, London, he and his men were facing three angels. When I next looked out on the street, the whole lot of them were gone. There was no way that Kozbar had gotten away from *angels*.

I shook my head. "He's dead. These guys might be connected to him, but he's toast."

She shrugged. "All right then. Come on. We have to get the others."

The "others" were a cross-section of kidnap victims from all over the continent. They were crammed into the old prison cells like sardines. The women ranged from early 20s to children. And there were boys, all prepubescent.

I felt the strong urge to kill the vampire pricks again.

Before we even went down to the prison, I made certain to clean Jillian's feet and give her the boots freshly vacated by their vampire owners. She was probably going to need more shots of consecrated antibiotics than I could guess just from being in this hellhole.

I also had Pearson search through the pocket litter of the dusty vampires as Jillian and I went to release the captives. I stopped guessing after the first two hundred women and boys were released. Pearson and I swept up our brass and made certain to pocket the magazines we dropped. I left my guns with Pearson and walked back to our car. I pulled the car up to the main building so we could put away our guns.

Lena and Adara were still asleep even as I started the car and shifted parking spaces.

Then, and only then, did we call the *politzei.*

Morderberg then became a three-ring circus of lights and sirens and vans and buses and calls to embassies. Some of the brass insisted we be arrested, but when there were no weapons on us, they had a problem. We informed them that we had recordings of our conversations with their police department, infuriating them even more.

Then the Nuncio from the Vatican Embassy showed up and started ripping the police a new one.

The *politzei* let us go. Despite all of the bureaucracy trying to come down on us, we were out of there at three in the morning.

Pearson and I carried Lena and Adara to a bedroom in the embassy. Pearson and I handed the embassy staff our clothing, since we were covered in asbestos, vampire dust, and other unmentionables.

We then collapsed.

The next morning, we were up at the crack of nine, since sunlight poured into my face at that point.

I was up, showered, and dressed by the time Pearson awoke. I was seated at a chair at the foot of his bed. His eyes opened, bleary and disoriented over where he woke up.

My first words to him were "Nazi Muslim vampires? Did I miss a memo?"

Pearson squinted at me. "And a happy good morning to you, too, Detective Nolan."

"I think it's time you explained a few things regarding last night."

Pearson shrugged. "What's to know? Vampires were on both sides of World War II—to be specific, they worked for the Nazis and the Soviets. The Waffen-SS had their own Muslim brigade. The 13th Waffen Mountain Division of the SS Handschar—or sword units. They were Bosnian Muslims, brought to you by Hitler's Mufti, Hajj Amin Al-Husseini. Since the Muslims and the vampires worked for the Nazis, I'm not all that surprised that we ran into a combination of them."

"Sacrificing a woman?"

Pearson rolled his eyes and fell back into bed. "I already told you, there were at least a dozen occult movements that the Nazis stole from for initiations into their pseudo-Odin cults. And would later hijack. Himmler had at least one dinner party where he took an ax off the wall and cut someone's head off so everyone could get some of the blood. So Islam was close to Hitler. Hitler worked on the occult. Now we have succubi and Asmodeus. Yay."

"And vampires?" I asked. "Where are they from? I ran into some trying to collect a bounty on me."

"They're from the same time period as the Soul Stone. Genesis. When giants walked the Earth. That sort of thing."

"I understand why they're Nazis, but why are they Jihadi vampires?"

"If you used concussive explosive vests, wouldn't you want a reusable suicide bomber?"

"Right ... Why did I even ask?"

"I don't know. If it makes you leave me alone for a few minutes, there are tickets I found in the pocket of one of the vampire's uniforms."

I rose from the chair and looked. The tickets were to a rock band named Poltergeist.

I rolled my eyes. *I guess they just couldn't call it Caspar the Friendly Ghost.*

The tickets were for that evening. It was over in Potsdam, just outside of Berlin.

I sat, studying what I could find on the internet about *Poltergeist*. There was very little...Except that it claimed to be Satanic. There was a photo of the lead singer, who dressed up like a neon-Pope meets Baron Samedi—his skull makeup was painted on with black light paint.

Is that what passes for the anti-Pope these days? Figures that theirs would have a lot of neon.

I couldn't help but chuckle. "I bet that if they saw a real demon, these little bitches would crap their pants."

Pearson sighed, stared up at the ceiling, then sat up, giving up the ghost. "I wouldn't be so sure of that, mate. This is Europe, inn'it? The land of Occult bollocks and frigging cults. A band like this provoked at least a few ritual sacrifices by their fans over the past thirty years. Then again, a *lot* of that is springing up. It's like the Devil was given the 20th century, and he took the time to lay seeds for the next one, too. Don't be surprised if a lot of these guys are at least a little possessed."

"A little possessed? Like having a bit of a head cold?"

Pearson shrugged. "Kinda. Demonic possession is usually nowhere near as dramatic as your man Curran, or even as dramatic as *The Exorcist* incident. Italy alone sees thousands of cases a year of demonic harassment. Mysterious, unexplained illnesses that go away with a quick blessing or a prayer. Intermittent pains and the demonic harassment of Voices that whisper in the mind. So any of these people could have a minor ... complaint, if you like."

Internally, I groaned at the thought of yet another fist fight with a demon. "Joy. Just... joy." I held up the tickets. "Why Potsdam?"

"It's thirty minutes away by car. It's considered a suburb of Berlin at this point, if we're honest. Why do you ask?"

"Because I was told by a dead witness in New York that the hub of the sex trafficking was Berlin. But if Potsdam is considered a suburb of the city—"

Pearson flinched. "An American may not know the difference. The hub of the sex trafficking may be there."

I nodded. "Time to kick some ass and take some names. Tonight—" I held the tickets up. "We hit a concert. With a hammer." I stood, energized to have a lead. "Let's go check on the girls."

I opened the door to the bedroom.

Lena and Adara were already there, waiting for us.

"You took forever," Lena told me.

I smiled. "We had a late night. You got to sleep through it." I looked at Adara. "I will need your grandfather's telephone number."

Adara blinked. "Why?"

"We have a location. He may need to make a delivery."

Adara gave me the number. I let Lena do the typing for the text message. The message was simple: "Delivery is needed. The location is Potsdam. Do you need anything?"

The reply was simple. Lena translated it as "Sachsenhausen."

I frowned and looked at Pearson. The priest answered, "It's a real place. Why? What are you and the Rabbi cooking up?"

I smiled. "Funny choice of words."

Lena tapped me on the hip with the phone, and I took it back. Lena stared at me petulantly for a moment, as only a 13-year-old could. "We want to come with you to the ghost band."

I arched my brows. "Oh, really?

"Yes. And if you don't bring us with you, you're gonna be sorry."

I automatically humored her—I did *not* want to see, in person, what the temper tantrum of a teenage telekinetic looked like. I had seen *Carrie*. "What would you do?"

Lena crossed her arms and looked stern and serious. "I am going to hold my breath until I turn blue."

After Pearson and I hit Mass, took communion, and were fed, both naturally and supernaturally Adara, Lena, and I played catch in the Nuncio's backyard. We varied between a baseball, a football (American, not European), and a soccer ball. It was in part to entertain the girls, in part to blow off some steam, and in part to exercise Lena's telekinesis. She didn't catch a single ball with her hands. It helped her with speed and accuracy since she was much more gentle throwing balls back to Adara than she was to me.

Lena didn't even break a window. That was Adara; that was my story if anyone asked. Thankfully, no one did.

After catch, Pearson called to check in with XO at the Vatican. Lena and Adara took a nap.

I called Mariel to give her an update on what had been going on.

She said, "Murder Berg? Really? The Soviets. So subtle."

"Tell me about it." I explained what happened there and what we found.

Mariel paused for a moment. "So you're going to a rock concert tonight with a rock band who wants to worship Satan. This should end well."

I chuckled. "Yeah. I know. We'll see how it goes."

We talked for a few more minutes, then hung up. I thought to settle in for the afternoon, catch up on rest before tonight's excursion. I collapsed into the temporary room they had set up for me. I rolled my eyes and let myself sleep.

THE BAND FOR POLTERGEIST WAS LED BY A HANS GAIMAN. According to his band page, Hans claimed to have been raised in a deeply-religious household, and his revenge was to sell his soul to Satan as a teenager and worship Satan as his god.

Despite everything I had seen and experienced since a demon broke up my precinct, I had to restrain myself from snickering at this idiot. It came from a long line of busts, ever since I was a patrolman, with idiot teenagers smoking pot and "worshiping Satan" in graveyards, usually with "sacrifices" they had gotten from the supermarket because no one wanted to play with trying to sacrifice an animal. The one person who had tried to sacrifice a cat had been scratched to heck and gone, losing the fight. So someone who was actually serious about this felt like a bad joke.

Though I guess I should approach this more like the Women's Health Corps death cult than some idiots in a graveyard.

Poltergeist didn't rate something the size of Madison Square Garden. It wasn't even Wacken, Germany (Yes, I am familiar with some of the bands that play there ... largely because of YouTube videos of the concerts there). The size of the hall was about the size of one of the moderate halls of Lincoln Center back home. It was big enough for a few hundred people.

We arrived early to get a sense of the layout. We wanted to be as prepared as possible. Unfortunately, we could only pack so many weapons in this situation. We were stuck with handguns. Between the rifles, paintball guns, and the shotguns, we could only take one of the long guns each. I went with a shotgun, and Pearson took a paintball gun. We figured that if there were metal detectors, we could circle back to the car and drop them off.

Pearson and I walked in with raincoats buttoned up. The men taking tickets at the front door didn't look at us twice, probably figuring us for perverts. They looked at Lena and Adara hungrily. Lena gave them both dirty looks but said nothing.

I wasn't surprised that these men both had a sniff of sin about them. Considering how my nose worked, that meant that they weren't just guys who watched a lot of porn at home.

After we walked past them, both ticket takers tripped over their own feet, while standing still.

Lena's dirty look turned into an evil little smile. If you don't know what I mean, you've never met a 13-year-old.

Our seats were in basically a box seat in the top row. It was strange, since none of the others were full.

The smell of sin slowly filled up the arena. With each wave that came in, there was a little more. At that moment, I guessed that either each group had several people who were minor evils, or one major evil per every ten or twenty people.

If the level of evil was akin to torturing animals, maybe half the audience was a problem. If it was a serial killer, then perhaps one in ten, or one in twenty. Either way, this spelled halfway decent odds if it came down to a fracas.

Eventually, the room filled. There were no chairs, so everyone stood, packed together so tightly I hope no one had asthma.

The audience was as colorful as you'd expect for this sort of band. They looked like KISS cosplayers—white face paint, black makeup around the eyes. No colors but black. Lots of leather.

Adara leaned over the rail, studying the audience. She asked, "Why are they dressed like that?"

"They really like Halloween and want it to be all year round," I answered honestly. Despite the branding, I didn't think most of the crowd was there for Satanic worship, especially if the smell meant anything.

The lights cut out suddenly. The children clung to me instantly. Their fear of the dark was either developed or enhanced by their container experience, so I didn't blame them.

"Don't worry," I told them. "If the dark comes to get you, I'll punch it in its face. Again." *It worked last time.*

The stage lights turned on ... though they were black lights, making the band appear as black cutouts, shadows on a black light background.

Except for the leader, Hans Gaiman. His skull face paint glowed blue in the blacklight. The outfit had a similar glow. The costume was a very ornate parody of the Pope's uniform, complete with hat and staff.

As I said, it was Baron Samedi meets neon Pope.

I was too busy to note all of those details at first glance. I was blasted with the smell of evil so hard, it felt like the stage was filled with a collection of demons. It knocked me back like I was hit.

Lena shook me a little. "Hussar!" she called over the music. "Are you all right?"

She grabbed my belt, as though I might go over the railing of our box.

I waved her off. "I'll get used to it."

Much to my surprise, it only got worse. I didn't understand the first song except for a chorus of "*Asmo-deus! Boph-amet! Luc-ifer!*" and "*Hail Satan!*" The crowd chanted along, adding to the power of the smell.

Pearson leaned over and spoke directly into my ear. "It's the crowd! They're feeding into a ritual of power. It's a ceremony, whether the audience knows it or not."

I ground my teeth. "How do we shut it down?" I asked back.

Pearson shouted back to me. "We'd have to shut down the

concert entirely. But I don't see how that will end well for us. Besides! With the group, I don't see it easily interrupted."

The first song ended. I fell back against the rail as though I had already been beaten around. Hans Gaiman spoke to the crowd in German.

Lena looked confused. "What sacrifice?" she asked.

I blinked. "Sacrifice?"

The woman was dressed in white, held by six men. Two were at each arm. Two were at her legs. Her ankles were tied together. She seemed less compliant than drugged.

An alter rose up on the stage. The woman was laid on it. There was a knife next to her.

I growled, pissed. "That's enough." I looked to Lena and hoped she could do what I needed her to. "Lena, pull their plugs."

Lena nodded. She moved towards the rail and stood up on the tips of her toes. She glared at the stage. The music had changed to a dirge with electronic instruments.

Then the wires for the electronic instruments were ripped out of their sockets and went flying. Wires smacked several of the group in the face. Their instruments went flying...right into the black lights, casting the entire house in darkness.

I took my cue and raced from the box seat, running along the second floor. I raced for the stage door. I kicked it in and unslung my shotgun in a guard's face. I shoved my way onstage in time for the house lights to come on.

Without the black light, Gaiman looked fairly goofy with the lights on and no glowing paint effects. KISS had nothing to fear.

"Politzei!" I bellowed for the room to hear.

That cut the party short. The crowd went dead silent.

The drummer charged me. Without a blink, I swiveled left and shot him in the chest. The buckshot blasted him off his feet.

"Suck it, Ringo," I muttered.

Gaiman looked at me. "Englander?"

"American," I barked. "Still politzei." I racked the shotgun and pointed it at the men holding the woman hostage. They untied her and ran off the stage.

Gaiman pointed at me with a finger and chanted in German.

Pearson called out from above. "Tommy! Shoot him! He's cursing you!"

Huh? I had been cursed at every day as a cop. What was the big deal?

Then the demons struck.

I was beaten soundly on the side of my head. The shotgun was knocked up to aim at the ceiling. Fists drove into my side—entire side, from my ankles to my hips, ribs, shoulders, and face. A backhand rocked me the other way. A swift kick to my balls lifted me off my feet, a foot off of the ground. I landed on my back. A heard of cats fell on me—that's what it felt like. I was scratched all over, my clothing offering no protection.

Except there was nothing visible attacking me, to heck with laying me out. I swung and connected with nothing but air. There was no defense because there was nothing there ... I only wished I could have convinced my body of that, too.

And the crowd cheered. "*Pol-ter-geist! Pol-ter-geist! Pol-ter-geist!*"

The half that believed in Gaiman's satanic powers cheered the beating of a cop. Those that didn't believe applauded a great performance on my part.

Gaiman swung over to point at Pearson and barked in German. Dozens from the crowd swept out, heading for the stairs, the priest, and the girls.

The guitarist came in as I tried to get up. I was on my knees when I blocked his kick with my shotgun. An invisible force struck me in my right ribs as the guitarist's right hook clocked me in the face. I swung the shogun like a club and swept his legs out from under him. He fell in front of me, and I was going to hammer him with the gun. But I was punched in the face by an unseen hand.

Hail Mary, full of grace—

An invisible uppercut slammed into my chin. I staggered backwards, to my feet. I was kicked in the hip, spinning me around.

Then the beating *really* started.

PEARSON WAVED THEM ONWARD. "COME ON, YA BLIGHTERS. Come at me if you think you're hard enough."

The first three came as a group, running straight for Pearson. Pearson's kick was meant to stop the leader, like kicking a door in. The sole of Pearson's shoe connected with his chest, knocking the leader back.

Pearson landed right foot forward, then swung right, opening up his hips as he drove a right hammer fist into the ear of the second man in formation. The blow knocked him sideways, as well as silly.

The satanist on Pearson's right caught up to them and swung an unwieldy roundhouse punch. Pearson ducked in a crouch and lunged, driving his fist into the satanist's gut with the full force of his body weight. The satanist bent over Pearson. The priest grabbed the attacker's wrist with his left hand and swung his right directly between the attacker's legs. With a sharp straightening of his spine and body, Pearson hefted the satanist and threw him into the man Pearson had hammered in the head. They both went down in a pile.

It had taken less than five seconds.

The first man had recovered, pulling out a knife, and the next two men in the group had joined him.

Pearson smiled as the adrenaline kicked in fully.

"I'm not the saint, my friend is," he said in German.

The satanists closed on him. The two fresh thugs closed in on his sides, and the leader with the knife came at him from the front. The leader also grinned, slowly closing, enjoying toying with the prey.

Except Pearson wasn't prey.

Pearson quickly made a two-step move that looked like a dance. He had gone from a passive, relaxed stance, feet spread, and burst left, sideways. His right foot landed first, his left foot right next to it. He raised his right knee up to his waist, then pivoted the left foot at the same time as he shot out with his right.

The sidekick into the knee of the man on the right collapsed the leg like an accordion that had an accident with a trash compactor.

Pearson delivered a knee to the man's face, then shoved past him.

The unconscious satanist collapsed between Pearson and his two friends.

The second thug hesitated, confused, but the leader didn't. He lunged for Pearson, trying to reach over his fallen comrade with the knife.

Pearson twisted his upper body, torquing his right side backwards, and parrying with his left hand. The knife went right past his body.

Pearson's hands clamped down on the wrist with the knife. He drove his thumbs into the back of the hand, folding over his hand so the palm bent towards the inside of the forearm. Pearson swung back with his left foot while twisting the arm counterclockwise.

The cracking sound that followed was the leader's arm enduring a spiral fracture as it broke in two places.

A quick hammer fist to the man's temple was enough to drop him to the floor.

The last man standing was paralyzed, confused, and bewildered at what happened.

Pearson wasted no time. He stepped on the pile of fallen satanists and leaped over them, his right fist cocked all the way back.

The fist drove into the last man's face before Pearson touched the ground, driving the full force of his body weight into an impact point around two square inches.

Pearson grinned.

Then he felt the pounding of the stairs as they charged for him and the girls.

"Father!" Lena called out. Pearson turned to her. She stepped out of the box and stood in the hall. "Save Hussar! I will stop them."

Pearson blinked. "Are you sure?"

The next group of satanists charged into the hallway.

Lena snapped around to face them. A square of drywall ripped out of the wall, swung around and smacked them in the face. The light fixtures above ripped out and swung down, shattering bulbs into their faces.

Pearson shrugged. "Never mind."

As Pearson was busy having fun with satanists, I was busy being assaulted by invisible forces, as well as the band Poltergeist. An invisible punch would send me into a punch from a real fist. First from the guitarist, then the keyboardist charged in. Then three backup dancers rushed to play.

Hans Gaiman stood back, smirking, which was wise. Despite being beset by five people, there was only room for three at a time.

The invisible force had ripped the gun out of my hands but not off of my shoulder. But it dangled there useless as I blocked incoming strikes from those I could see.

Then the knife came out. The guitarist held it and pulled it out right in front of me. He slashed it for my face, and I leaned back. A dancer on my right punched for my face, and I blocked it. The dancer on my left kicked my hip at the same time, bending me over sideways.

I grabbed the dancer's foot at the ankle to take him out of play, but the one behind me grabbed me by the shoulder and threw me into the guitarist's knife. The knife came in from below, like an uppercut.

I blocked the knife with the dancer's leg. It drove through the calf muscle. I shoved the leg behind me. The leg took the knife with it. I grabbed the guitarist and spun him around, into his dancer friend. I drove a knee into the guitarist's gut.

Then I was smacked in the face by an invisible hand. The guitarist shoved me away.

The third dancer kicked me in the back. I dropped to my knees.

Holy Mary, Mother of God, pray for us sinners.

Both dancers pulled knives.

Now and at the hour of our deaths.

Without any warning, I was struck in the chest three times. There was a *splat* each time, and my chest was covered in water.

The band members laughed at me.

Then Gaiman was spattered several more times.

I dropped to my hands and knees, missing a knife slash from behind me.

I vomited.

The only thing that came up were nails.

Nails? I briefly wondered.

The guitarist in front of me said something, and I charged forward, driving my shoulder into his knee. The kneecap *slid* inside of his leg, ripped out of place by my shoulder. He screamed as he went down.

I roared to my feet and whirled around as the second dancer charged me with the knife. He held it upside down, like an ice pick in his right hand.

I chopped for the incoming satanist, the blade of my hand slamming into his throat. He dropped his knife and grabbed for his throat. I grabbed him by the hair and threw him into the crowd.

I turned to the last dancer and the keyboardist...

I swung the shotgun up to my shoulder and fired one to the face of the dancer and the other to the keyboardist.

I wheeled around to the band leader.

"Haaaaaaaans!" I roared.

Gaiman looked at me, then down at his front. He glanced to the balcony.

Father Pearson held his paintball gun. He had blasted both of us with holy water, one to protect me from the curse, the other to prevent the curse from being sustained.

I was slammed from the side by fans who clambered on stage in defense of their band leader.

I twisted, smacking one in the skull with the shotgun. I fired into the attackers. I cycled through the magazine as I cut into the horde.

Gaiman laughed as I killed his followers.

The magazine fell out of the shotgun as I ran out of shells, and he ran out of followers.

I turned to Gaiman, and he was already on me with his anti-Papal staff. I blocked an overhead strike but took another blow to the side with the opposite end of his staff.

I cringed, looping my arm around the center of the staff. I pulled it up against me, reared back, and crashed my forehead into his nose. Gaiman staggered a little and let go of the staff. I reached over with both hands, grabbed him by the shoulders, and head-butted him again. He staggered, knees going weak.

I drove my elbow into his face, crushing his nose. I hammered him in the side of his head, making him falter, then fall. I ripped the staff away from him, and called out, in a voice and tone that crossed language barriers, "You're under arrest!"

The crowd that had stared on in stunned complaisance grew restless and unruly. It could have been as good, law-abiding Germans, they couldn't abide having the authority (in this case, the band) be beaten, conflicted with the innate kowtowing to authority (the *politzei*) ... then again, Europe was the land of people who objected to the "Americanization of soccer games" when the food improved, the seats were comfortable, and that soccer riots had all but vanished.

Maybe they feel the urge for a soccer game to start.

I reached for my shotgun, ready to reload.

Then the main doors to the hall exploded inwards. It was a *politzei* tactical team, complete with battering ram and machine guns.

Leading their way was Kommissar Berger, the cop from the Munich nightclub.

I found myself with Gaiman's staff in one hand and placed it on the stage.

Suddenly, all of my injuries caught up to me. I had fought through them with adrenaline and willpower. Now, with the cops arrived, my body decided that right then was the perfect time to collapse. My knees buckled, my hips felt disjointed, my ribs were bruised up one side and down the other. I grabbed Gaiman's staff with both hands, using it to support myself.

Berger's team threw everyone standing up against the wall while Berger himself headed straight for me. His face hadn't lost his hangdog expression. I idly wondered if there was anything that could make him get a different facial expression. He had a Glock in one hand and a lit cigarette in another.

"Kommissar Nolan!" he called casually. "Funny to see you here."

I tried to shrug nonchalantly, but it hurt too much. "I get around."

Berger nodded as he surveyed the stage filled with the bodies of band and fans. "So I see."

I looked him up and down. Nothing phased him. "Long way from Munich, though, aren't you?"

Berger gave a sad little smile, and his eyes lit up a little without making him seem more awake. *Cute trick, that.* "Oh, I'm sorry. You thought I was with, what? Vice, perhaps? Homicide?" He shook his head. "I believe you would call me the Occult Squad. I..." he drifted off as he looked at me. "Oh good God."

I looked down. My white shirt was stained up and down with blood.

"This might be bad," were my last words before I passed out.

I spent the evening with a collection of nuns who used to run hospitals in other countries but had been kicked to the curb by governments who decided that they preferred socialized medicine to inexpensive religious folks.

I was diagnosed with a case of blood loss and a more severe case of exhaustion. My body was covered with scratches that looked like I had gone one-on-one with the entire big-cats section of the zoo. My face was bruised and scratched, with little white patches of skin here and there that were untouched. My neck was the same. Below the neck, however, my body was either bruised or bandaged. The nurse nuns told me to not move for the better part of the next week, and to drink like a fish—nothing but water and juice, something to offset the entire pint of blood they estimated I'd lost.

When I woke up in the rectory the next morning, Lena sat by my bed. She was asleep, but her eyes snapped open and glared around the room, as though she dared have someone approach me.

"Hi," I croaked. *Confirmed. I sound as bad as I feel.*

Lena's face snapped towards me and she beamed. "Hussar! Good."

I smiled at her faintly. "You can call me Tommy, you know."

Lena shook her head vehemently. "No. You are Hussar. You come to the rescue. You just need the wings."

It took me a moment to connect to the Winged Hussars, the Polish mounted cavalry that had decorative wings on the back of their armor. They were best known for saving Vienna from the Sultan's forces at one of the sieges. Which was appropriate, as I felt like I had been through the Siege of Vienna.

I smiled weakly. "I'm surprised that Berger left me alone."

The door creaked opened. Berger walked in, cigarette in one hand, wastebasket in the other. "Sorry to disappoint you."

Lena said, pouting. "He was waiting outside all night."

I raised my eyebrows. Most detectives wouldn't wait all night for a suspect to get patched back together. They would typically put a uniformed officer on station and wander off to do something else until summoned. The uniform was a sentry and a pager system.

My smile flickered at her. "It's his job. Mine, too, technically."

Berger nodded. "Yes, but your job is thousands of miles away." He hopped up on top of a small desk, one foot on the chair. He flicked the ashes from his cigarette into the wastebasket. "And you are the last witness statement I need to collect before this report gets put to bed."

My eyes narrowed. I couldn't believe that the bodies of at least a dozen people could be swept under the rug that easily. "How?"

Berger shrugged. "Most of the dead are, how would you say, career criminals?" He smiled evilly. "All very bad men."

Uh huh. Right. "Why do I feel like I'm cleaning up your back-log? You said something about an occult squad?"

Berger gave a casual shrug again. "Correct."

"I thought that was an 80s thing?"

"Maybe in America, Kommissar Nolan. But in Europe, the occult is on the rise, and they are not shy. In Italy, they've had decades of problems. And by occult, we do not mean the, um... hippy-dippy new-age *Ficken*. We mean satanism. Self-mutilations, destruction of private property. Teenage girls who stab nuns to death in satanic rituals. The *Bestie di Satana* were tried for killing three people, including one of their own. I am particularly fond of the man with amnesia who walked into a police station in Milan covered in needle marks, missing three liters of blood—the blood was used for satanic finger painting on the walls of his apartment over seventy miles away. The man had no recollection of belonging to a cult, and no idea of how he went from place to place."

Berger shrugged again and leaned back on the desk, causing it to creak. He gave it no mind as he took another drag on the cigarette. "You can blame the Enlightenment. Satan rebelling against God was a symbol of *freedom*. Ha! Back then, they used it to form clubs for orgies. Now? Killings. We're not the only ones who do it. The UK police have a special task force to track occult cases, but they don't like to discuss it. The SAS even has a priest on call to consult on satanism, though no one knows his name."

I blinked, taken aback. Father Michael Pearson, he of the British accent, called himself a "combat exorcist." I wondered what he was doing when he wasn't gallivanting around with me.

"Why didn't you tell me you were Occult Squad?"

Berger's sleepy smile turned cynical. "How do you put it? We get no respect." He tapped ashes into the wastebasket again. "I think you and I should talk, Herr Kommissar Nolan."

I sighed and forced myself into a seated position in the bed. Berger winced at the sight of my naked chest, covered in bruises and bandages. I didn't blame him, it hurt me just to do it. "Just Tommy."

Berger nodded. "Okay then, Tommy. Should I ask what you are doing at a satanic rock band with two children and a priest?"

I smiled. "I couldn't get a babysitter for any of them. Pearson's especially hard to shop for."

Berger's head tilted like a curious German shepherd annoyed at what was being offered him. "Be serious."

I tried to shrug, but it hurt too much. "If you insist. You may have heard of the Morderberg bust?"

Berger nodded. He didn't say anything more for a long moment. Neither did I. If he knew I was there, I was going to have him admit it. After a long moment, he said, "I know you freed a large collection of people who had been kidnapped and enslaved for sex trafficking."

"We found evidence pointing to the concert as a matter of interest to the traffickers. So it was a matter of interest to me."

Berger's eyebrows went up, without his eyes opening wider. "And you did not point it out to the Berlin *politzei* because?"

I rolled my eyes and stiffly reached for the glass of water at my nightstand. Lena hopped down from the chair, grabbed a pitcher and glass, poured, and handed it to me. I took a sip that consumed half the glass. I didn't try to put it back, since that required effort. Lena carefully topped off the glass. I smiled at her, and she moved back to the chair.

"I didn't tell them because it wasn't my job. The first thing they tried to do was arrest me."

"For?" Berger asked.

"Weapons charges," I told him. I was suddenly concerned with the shotgun on my back when Berger had broken into the Poltergeist concert. "But they didn't find any on me at the time."

Berger nodded. "I imagine not."

I waited for more. He took a drag on the cigarette, held the breath, and slowly let it out. He smiled at me in his sleepy manner. He wanted me to fill the vacuum of noise.

Well, if he's not going to mention it, neither am I. We can both play this game. I sipped. "Next question?"

"Why follow up with Poltergeist? Hmm? Did you not find all of the parishioners in Morderberg?"

I did my best not to react to that. I hadn't even asked Pearson how many of the women and boys we'd found were Catholic, and who wasn't. I hadn't cared who was a member of our tribe, and who wasn't. I probably should have inquired.

"Too easy," I answered. "We're less here about the Catholics kidnapped than we are the ring itself. We want it shut down. All of it. The only way to do that is to do it ourselves."

Berger sighed, suddenly exhausted. "You might be more correct than you realize, Kom.... Tommy."

"Thanks, but I've already gotten the picture that the cops in Europe are pretty damn useless."

Berger stopped in mid-puff and slowly let the smoke curl out from his nostrils. He kept his face impassive, the way I would when I wanted to reserve judgment before reacting. "Would you care to explain that particular assessment?"

I sipped deliberately, drawing out the silence. Berger's eyes narrowed. He knew I was doing it deliberately. We were two cops playing the same game with each other that we had played on dozens of suspects in the past.

"To be polite, let's start with my trip to London. What is *Rotherham* in German?"

Berger winced but said nothing in defense of a sex trafficking ring that was allowed to operate for decades through both political correctness and police corruption.

I continued. "Look, in the UK they were not only actively *allowing* Islam to trample the law, but some of them were also in bed with them. Bigwig government hot shots and corrupt cops were in with a radical psychopath named Kozbar."

Berger's posture shifted. He shot up straight, he held the cigarette off to one side. He placed the wastebasket next to him on

the desk. His eyes even opened all the way. "Kozbar? *Imam*
Kozbar?"

I think I hit a sore spot. "Old friend?"

Berger spat in the basket. "I'd give *body parts* to arrest him.
Perhaps even some of my own."

I smiled. I liked Berger when he was awake. "Sorry. It'll never
happen."

Berger sighed and sagged back on the desk. "I know. I know.
Europol is useless. Interpol is a glorified bulletin board." He
flicked some ash into the garbage, incensed. "Bah. Useless. All
of us."

"No," I corrected him. "You'll never arrest him. He's facing a
higher authority. Technically, he already has."

Berger perked up. "Oh, really? Good."

"Happy to give you the good news," I told him. "How did
Kozbar get your attention?"

Berger shrugged and resettled himself so he was less casual
and more ready to get back to business. "The nightclub you broke
up was under suspicion because people would go in and not come
out. The few survivors who came out described sex rites and rituals, demons, all of which are in my purview. I said we lost police in
the club, but our external surveillance caught Kozbar as one of the
few who went in and came out without any ill effects. After we
lost our people, we were pulled off by government cronies who
didn't want to offend a small business owner and an Imam."

"Kozbar knew you were watching the club," I concluded.

Berger nodded. "We concluded that our men were caught and
made to talk. We kept tabs on Kozbar but could prove nothing. He
made a visit to these Poltergeist people, which we found out only
because we had Poltergeist under a separate surveillance."

I could feel the puzzle pieces moving together. Kozbar, Fowler,
and Toynbee were tied to the sex trafficking. Somehow, the
succubus Jayden was... working for Kozbar? And somehow, raising

Asmodeus was a part of all of this? Kozbar had been setting it up for months. The bokor, Baracus, had been tied together with all of this. Kozbar had wanted his advice on both the German situation and the Soul Stone. Baracus had told me that he was informing on the German operation because the check had bounced—perhaps it was also because everyone who tied him to the German operation was already dead? Baracus had taken his money and left Fowler's side before I had come on the scene.

Fowler's check hadn't bounced, I concluded.

There were still pieces missing. And I wanted all of them. "Can I talk with Gaiman?"

Berger shrugged. "If you like. He should be out of the hospital by now. We've got enough on him for a dozen murders and conspiracy. Apparently, last night was not the first person he sacrificed on stage, in front of hundreds of people. When we explained that to their fans, many of them were eager to spell out details of what they thought had been a staged sacrifice."

I frowned. The sad thing was that it wouldn't be that hard to convince people that they were watching a staged murder. Unless someone had perfect eyesight, a front-row seat, and a great mind for faces, Poltergeist could have murdered one woman each night, and as long as they had another woman, dressed the same way, with similar hair, show up after each performance, they could pass it off as an act.

"What more could you want from them?" Berger asked.

"I want to know how they fit with Kozbar. Why kill people? Pearson said something about a ritual of power."

Berger nodded. "It is a thing. Mass gatherings, using the energy of the crowd to gather power. Couple that with human sacrifice, it would be a powerful weapon. Some say that was the point of Hitler's public appearances—gather the energy of thousands for victory." He smiled like a man telling ghost stories around the camp fire. "Though once Hitler stopped holding the rallies, his regime started falling apart. Funny that." Berger hopped down from the desk. "Thank you. I'm going to arrange a meeting with Gaiman. You rest. You're going to need it."

Berger opened the door and paused. He looked at me and said, "Oh, while I think about it, Father Pearson has all of your personal possessions. All of them."

That answers my questions about the guns. "Thanks."

Berger went out, and Pearson came in. Lena grabbed my glass and topped it off again. She thrust it back at me and said, "Drink."

I drank. Pearson smiled at the exchange. He sat at the foot of the bed. "Good to see you're still up and alive."

I put down the glass, and Lena refilled it again. "So far. Give me time."

Pearson looked over my bruised chest. "You had a rough go of it."

"No kidding. What was it? Was Gaiman telekinetic?"

Pearson shook his head. "He cursed you. When you vomited? That was the curse being removed. It happens."

I thought back to the fight. "They were nails. How did that not rip up my insides?"

"Every instance of cursing I've seen has had the materials spring into existence *inside* the mouth, not down in the stomach. Notice they melted away. That usually happens, too. I've seen ribbons, nails, little dolls. Very nasty stuff."

I paused a moment. "I'd thought that curses caused internal problems."

Pearson shrugged. "That also happens. But you're the first case of demonic assault and battery that I've seen for a few years."

I blinked. "Excuse me?"

Pearson shrugged. "Oh yeah, it's happened, even to saints. They've been assaulted, beaten, scratched, bruised, slapped, beaten half to heck and back?"

I sighed. "Great. Just great."

Lena poked me. She was still several feet away, sitting in the chair. "Drink."

I drank.

Pearson smiled at the exchange. "You get some rest. When Berger calls, we'll come wake you."

Pearson woke me up several hours later. Berger had arranged the interview for that afternoon. I had two hours to get up, dressed, fed, and down to the police station.

I tried moving. It didn't work. It hurt to breathe. It hurt to stay horizontal. It hurt to turn my head. The only reason I had managed to sleep was partially because of sedatives and partially because I was exhausted. After I had been beaten half to death by my first demon, I was laid up for the better part of a month. This felt worse.

I took a deep breath and slowly let it out. I went through my morning offering—an Our Father, a Hail Mary and a Glory Be. I followed it up with something simple and straightforward.

Hi, God. Sorry I didn't get to Mass this morning. I'd say it was because I'm in agony, but I really just slept in. I know it would take no effort on your part to get me moving again, but that feels like cheating. Right now, I just need to get out of bed, get dressed, and get to the police station. All I ask is to be healed for as much as I need for as long as I need. I don't want or need to bounce back like I'm a comic book character. All I need is to go from point A to B, talk a little, and listen. I may merely be asking for the equivalent of an Advil, but I honestly hurt too much to reach for one. I'm going to try to get up now. Please help. Thanks. Amen.

I swung my legs over and let the momentum take me up to my feet. My joints creaked and groaned. I staggered to the rest room, pissed blood, and drank some more.

Thanks again, God. Movement is going to help.

I slowly made my way back to the bedroom, going through prayers in my head. I wanted to make up for missing Mass that morning. Also, if I kept concentrating on prayer, I felt less pain. Some people need to be Yoga masters to meditate and tune out pain. I just need the rosary- and the Sorrowful Mysteries in my head to remind me that He had had it worse

The bag of personal effects was left on the lamp table. I slipped on my wedding ring first, the Soul Ring second. It was tempting to test the new toy to see if it could do things other than act as a weapon of mass destruction, but I was mobile. God granted me the ability to move through the pain or suppress the pain; I would take what I could get and move on. I would also take Advil as soon as I could, since using my gifts to do the same job as medication just seemed self-indulgent.

Another reason not to use the Soul Ring—I had seen what it could do in the wrong hands, or used for the wrong reasons. Erring on the side of caution made good survival sense.

I considered a T-shirt, but that required getting my arms over my head. I went for a button- down and left off the tie. This wasn't going to be the day for it. We'd be visiting a police station in a country where I wasn't allowed to carry a gun, so we'd have to leave the weapons behind.

Lena saw me and raced to my side. Adara joined her, making certain that I didn't fall down the stairs. I was going to tell them that I didn't look that bad, but it occurred to me that it would be a lie. I looked worse than I felt. If I saw someone who looked like me walking down the street, I'd want to confirm whether or not it was a zombie.

Pearson saw me and the girls, and rushed to my side. "Good God, Detective. Are you sure you should even be moving?"

I gave him a flicker of a smile. "Do you think this is going to get better if I stay in bed for the next week? Because if the bad guys are going to take a few days off from kidnapping innocent people, I'll happily go back to bed."

Pearson frowned and said, "Give me your arm and rest your weight on me."

From the moment I sat down to eat until the moment we walked into the police station, the three of them watched me like a cat trying to win a staring contest. I ignored them all and tried to move normally, or at least as normally as my body would allow. I was allowed to carry nothing in my hands. Lena carried a gallon of water with us, since she took seriously the admonition that I should be drinking regularly. Adara carried the other gallon with both hands.

When I arrived at the police station, Berger took one glance at me and said, "You look terrible."

"Yes I do. Where's Gaiman?" I asked.

I was led to the interrogation room. Berger stopped us before I went in. "I will only allow two of you to go in. Gaiman is chained to the table. We will be videotaping everything that is said in there."

I didn't shrug or nod as I wanted to. It hurt too much. "Keep in mind, anything he says, I'm just going to roll with. He starts going on about demons, I'm just going to play along. Okay?"

Berger nodded. "Of course."

"Okay. Lena is coming in with me."

Berger blinked and took a moment to figure out what I was saying. He pointed to her. "This Lena?"

I nodded. "I'll need a translator. And I don't think we can

talk her out of coming in with me." I smiled. "Look at it this way, between the video, my current condition, and her build, you know that we won't be working him over with a phone book."

Berger's brows furrowed. "Why would you?"

I rolled my eyes. "It's just an expression."

Lena and I moved into the interrogation room. Hans Gaiman was less impressive without his neon anti-Pope outfit. He looked like a sad, bland little man with few stand-out facial features. And a bad case of acne.

"You," he muttered. "What do you want?"

I was taken aback. *I didn't know he spoke English. I'm surprised that Berger didn't bring it up when I said Lena would translate.*

"I'm going to ask you questions. You're going to answer them."

Gaiman sneered at me. "Or what?"

"Or I'll let her ask you questions. However she wants. Ever see *Firestarter?*"

Gaiman looked at Lena and snickered. "Her? Please. Stupid little girl—"

The chair slipped out from under Gaiman, dropping his butt to the floor. But since he was chained to the table, the chains caught him before he could drop all the way—and the table was bolted to the floor.

"Oops," I said blandly. "You should be more careful. Especially with what you say. She can be scary when you upset her."

Gaiman took a moment to get his legs under him and get to his feet. He looked at Lena curiously, clearly suspecting that she was trouble.

"Are you going to answer questions," I asked, "or will Lena have to take over?"

Gaiman frowned, though it looked more like a pout. "Okay. Okay. Ask."

"What's been going on with the sacrifices?" I asked. "The kidnapping."

Gaiman snagged his chair back with his foot, dragged it over, and sat. "Some taxis will take people away. To the outskirts of Potsdam."

I winced. In the Rotherham incident in England, taxi cabs would also kidnap their fares and ferret them away to the rape house.

"Where in Potsdam?" I asked casually.

He shrugged. "I don't know. Why would I?"

I refrained from reacting. "And the sacrifices? Where do they fit?"

"It's all for the same goal. Different types of sacrifices. To raise one of the *great lords of Satan*."

Even his delivery of the line was over the top. But I wanted to belittle his knowledge and how deep he was in the conspiracy. I wanted to make him think he was low man on the totem pole. "Yeah, yeah, Asmodeus. Been there, done that, heard it already." I hesitated only briefly, considering what I wanted to tell him, balanced off of what I could say in front of Berger. "From a succubus named Jayden."

Gaiman's eyes lit up with unholy fervor. His smiled became intoxicated, with a touch of psychotic thrown in. "Ah! Jayden! That is what we call her, but her name is greater. She is one of the Children of Lilith."

I nodded slowly, trying not to hurt myself. Pearson had said something about Lilith and succubi earlier. "I like how you capitalized the words there just by speaking. Honestly, what's the point of the sex trafficking? Who's behind it?"

Gaiman reared back as far as the chains would allow. He was a dog awakened from a nap who just heard the mailman. "The great Imam Kozbar, of course. He is one of the descendants of the Great Mufti Hajj Amin Al-Husseini."

"He was the Grand Mufti," I corrected him, remembering Pearson's lecture from before. "Of Jerusalem, not the great Mufti. Hitler's Mufti."

Gaiman grinned like a loon. "Yes! Al-Husseini had left a journal. Notes on plots he and Himmler worked on together. And Husseini's best friend, Eichman. They needed sexual sacrifices to our lord and master—!"

I interrupted him to break the flow of his ranting. I waved all of that away with a dismissive flick of my wrist from the table. It may have been the only joint that didn't hurt... much. "Yeah, yeah, I get it. Still unimpressed. Whatever it is you're doing, you need rape. Lots of it. Lots of women. And boys. Lots of men doing it. Who's running it all?"

Gaiman paused, confused. "Kozbar, of course."

Time to drop the hammer. "Kozbar's dead."

Gaiman shrugged, like he didn't care. How could he, next to Jayden. "I didn't know that. One of the journals allowed Kozbar to raise a lesser demon. Someone he believed he, or any of his followers, could control."

I flinched. "Jayden. She's under Kozbar's 'control,' and *she's* running it?"

"Well, if Kozbar's dead, so of course she's running it."

I frowned, sitting back for a moment as I considered everything Gaiman had said. *Jayden was raised by Imam Kozbar because she could be "controlled." Demons can be summoned and ordered via compulsions. But that would mean that Jayden is running the sex ring under compulsions Kozbar left behind months ago. Kozbar figured that he would play the Fowlers in London, while the German sex ring ran without him. The compulsions that Jayden is now might even be refreshed by Kozbar's minions—and the minions were told to let it run automatically until ... what? What was the end point?*

"So, what?" I asked. "This ring of sex slavery and human sacrifice just goes on and on until..."

Gaiman nodded, smiling. "The built up power caused by the sex ring will reach critical mass, please Asmodeus, and unleash an army of demons on Germany! Then and only then will our lord and master, Asmodeus be released!"

Internally, the idea horrified me. Tangling with one riot driven by demons was bad enough. If these demons were physically manifested, that would be nightmarish. Externally, I scoffed, "Bull. I don't believe that they'd need someone like you."

Gaiman sneered. "We supply more fodder for the altars. We donate blood to the cause. Some of it is even our own."

Okay, that made sense. Every drop helps. "Why Jayden? Why a succubus? Why raise several?"

Gaiman laughed. "Because cops can't question a *demon*. They'd never break under questioning, assuming the stupid cops could even subdue them. And the succubi help break the sacrifices."

I blinked, slightly confused. "I thought you drugged them before your sacrifices."

Gaiman rolled his eyes, thinking me a moron. "Not *my* sacrifices, the ones brought to the Potsdam house, to be properly groomed for their role as whores for Asmodeus. The succubi *make* them enjoy what happens. After the first dozen orgasms forced out of them by the demons, it's harder for them to resist the next dozen. After a while, the ones being groomed become sex addicts. They can't stop. They want it, they enjoy it." He smirked. "They're willing to do anyone who asks."

Despite how much it would hurt me to do it, I braced myself so I could leap across the table and punch Gaiman in his stupid, satanic-worshiping face.

The chair slipped out from under Gaiman again. This time, he dragged the heavy metal table down on top of him. I blinked and looked down. The bolts attaching the legs to the floor had been unscrewed.

I looked to Lena. She smiled at me and shrugged. I reached over and patted her gently on the head. "Good girl."

An assortment of *politzei* came in to help Gaiman to his feet and reset the table. Pearson came in and helped me to my feet.

When I was firmly secured around his shoulders, Pearson whispered, "If you knew how to speak fluent German this entire time, why did you have me and Lena translate for you?"

I frowned, confused, "I don't speak German. I'm too used to using Spanish. What do I need German for in my neck of Queens, I'm not in Maspeth."

"Funny. You were speaking fluent German just now."

After the interview with Hans Gaiman, Kommissar Berger had the what (sexual slavery), when (for the last few months), and how (kidnapping across the continent and via taxi cabs).

Unfortunately the "who", "why" and the "where" were too vague or too insane.

"Where" was a big house in Potsdam. That didn't narrow it down enough for a search grid, to heck with a search warrant.

The "who" was ... insane. Sure, occultist Jihadis led by a succubus summoned from the depths of Hell are kidnapping European citizens. And, according to the Polish tactical team who led the raid on the succubi in Krakow, succubi didn't have finger-prints, and there was only one name on the apartment—so if Jayden had a real name and identity with which to track her, no one knew it.

This didn't include everything else that had happened along the way, including vampires.

The real question should have been how to find the Potsdam house in question.

Instead, the question became how to get the wheels moving to even *find* the house in question. Because cops have three natural enemies—our own stupidity, criminals, and government bureau-cracy. The first two we can usually fight on our own. The crimi-nals were our job. Fighting our own stupidity and laziness became second nature (every cop can find at least one other cop who does not, cannot, or will not do their job—and find ways to work around them when need be). The bureaucracy usually came in the form of paperwork that we needed to plow through, eating up man hours we'd rather be using on the street.

In Germany, much to my surprise, the bureaucracy would actually come straight to the precinct and interrupt work.

The politician's rant was boring and easily skipped. He might as well have sent a record—"Islam is a religion of peace, they would never operate a sex slavery operation" (it still operated in Africa, run by Islam, but no one told him that); "this witness is insane, just charge him" (actually, his motivations were insane. His actions were clearly spelled out; so why dismiss all of the addi-tional crimes he was charged with?). Additional ranting included insulting "the American troublemaker," but that rant was cut short when Lena telekinetically smacked him from across the room. He made his excuses and fled, not wanting to discuss the unseen force that had assaulted him.

The energy in the room had gone from "Let's mount up and hunt us some bad guys" to "Damn it" in the space of a few minutes.

I took Pearson's hand, and he helped me to my feet. I creaked to the front of the conference room where the bureaucrat had gathered the detectives in order to demoralize everyone. Berger helped me forward, hoping I could say something to the troops.

I could only imagine what I looked like to them. I was bruised. My hands were scarred.

I waved at them and said to Pearson under my breath, "If the next words out of my mouth aren't German, translate."

I smiled at them as best I could. "Everyone. Hi. Those of you who don't know me, I am Detective Thomas Nolan from America, the NYPD to be precise. If you do not know, with the help of Father Michael Pearson here, we broke up the nightclub in Munich that had disappeared several police officers and rescued sex slaves from all over the continent. We made our way to Morderberg in Berlin and did the same thing there, after the slavers had killed two police officers. Obviously, we're part of the reason the band Poltergeist is currently in jail. Like the rest of you, I heard the total and complete bullshit from the bureaucrat who came in here and bitched us all out. He said you could not go out and do your jobs. He said you could not go door to door. He said you cannot canvass neighborhoods. He said you couldn't question witnesses.

"What he *did not say* was simple. What he *did not say* was clear." I paused. Pearson didn't translate, so my newly found gift of speaking in foreign tongues and being understood was currently working. "He *did not say* you couldn't talk to your fellow police officers. He *did not say* you couldn't find beat cops, bring them in, and ask them what they know."

The cops around me looked confused for a moment. "You're all detectives!" I told them. "And the cop on the street will know things already that we don't. When this happened in Rotherham, the sex slavery was an open secret. Citizens came in and complained to the cops. They were told that they were white supremacists, racists, and they were told that Islam is a religion of peace and that *such things couldn't happen here.*"

I emphasized the last phrase because it had special ramifications in Germany. I paused and let everyone in the room give each other a look of *"He did not just say that"* before I continued. "In that situation, it was an open secret, kept away from the spotlight by political correctness and corrupt cops. My suggestion to you, and to Detective Berger, is to go to the precincts. Go through the files. To talk to the beat cops. Find the citizens who came to the cops and were dismissed. Because I guarantee you that they're out there. I tell you now that if you look, you will find them.

"Now, I'm new here. I am from out of town. I am a stranger to you. But where I come from, we do our jobs without fear or favor. We do not favor criminals because of their religion or their skin colors, and we don't fear the politicians and their power. We know —everyone in this room knows—that we are on crusade. Every day, we are in a war on crime and criminals. No matter what."

"Why not just say that God wills it?" a cop in the back snickered.

I threw right back. "God *does* will it. God is the God of justice and freedom. These jerks are slavers and rapists. Death is too good for them! *Justice* demands it."

"Crusader nutjob!" the same cop heckled.

"*Deus vult,*" I snarked right back at him.

I was going to say something else, but I had to grab the desk. I became faint. I wondered what was going on, then I looked at the Soul Ring. It was glowing amber. I reached over with my thumb and turned it upside down so no one else could see it. I was also worried that it was ready to fire. I didn't know what the color amber meant, but, in case it was ready to fire, I hoped that turning it in towards the palm would prevent it from shooting off.

But the rest of the room was silent as well. For a moment, I thought that it was my words that had swayed them. I glanced off to the side at Pearson and Berger. Both of them ran the fingers up and down their shirt buttons. I looked down to the front of my own shirt. Blood patches were seeping through at several points in my shirt.

Another shirt ruined. I'm glad I go for the cheap crap on sale.

I mentally shrugged. *I guess even German cops will respect a guy who will stand up and bleed through work.* I faced the room and said, "Pardon me. I seem to have wet myself."

There was some uncomfortable laughter from the hecklers in

the back. There were three guys who gave hearty laughs closer up front, applauding that I made a joke out of bleeding.

Berger opened the door for me and whispered, "Go outside, then make a right down the hall to our nurse's station."

I gave a tight, controlled little nod as I strode outside. *Don't faint. Don't faint. Please God, don't let me faint in front of these people. I'll drink more. Honest.*

I was out of sight of the *politzei* bullpen before I fell against the wall outside. *Okay Lord, this will suck. But just let me get to the nurse's station. I can fall over there. Passing out will just make me look wimpy.*

Pearson and Lena swooped in and caught me before I hit the floor. "Thanks for waiting," I said weakly. *Lord, how much have you been holding me together? Or should I not ask these questions?*

Pearson flashed me a smile. "Of course. Can't look weak in front of the Germans. That's not how we did it during the war."

I gave him a small smile. "I thought how you did it during the war was to wait for the Americans to come and save your asses. Again."

"Don't be cheeky."

The nurse took one look at my shirt, and she went nuts. She chased Pearson and Lena out and got other cops to help get me into a glorified dentist's chair. Every bandage on my body was soaked with blood. It took the better part of an hour, but I was re-wrapped before shift change. Cops being cops, everyone had heard about my beaten, bruised and bloody condition before shift change was over. I was redressed with clothes that weren't covered in blood by cops in the station who were happy to donate backup clothing to the cause. This meant I was dressed in a navy blue sweatsuit.

I started on praying the rosary. I was two decades in when I fell asleep in the middle of a *Hail Mary*. But don't worry, my guardian angel was up to the task of finishing it.

When I woke up, Lena was next to me. Again. She moved quietly for a child. Jeremy preferred to stampede.

"Hussar, you're not going to die are you?"

I blinked, confused. "Hopefully, not for a long, long time. If you're worried about the blood and bruises, no. They shouldn't kill me. They're just going to slow me down for a while."

Lena nodded slowly, thoughtfully. "Okay."

I tried to shift in my seat, but couldn't. "Lena, you realize that you can't abuse everyone who makes you angry, don't you? What you've done today was good, and it was for a purpose." I paused a moment. "Okay, the bureaucrat *may* not have deserved it, but I'll give you a pass on that. But that's not something you should do on a day-to-day basis. You realize that, don't you?"

Lena frowned. "I know. But he shouldn't have talked like that."

"No. He shouldn't. But adults can be stupid. Doesn't mean you strike all of them. No matter how much one may like to. Okay?"

"Okay."

"Okay." I paused and I felt the need to bring up another point. "Now, while you've helped me and Pearson out a lot on this case, we're almost at a point where the problems that face us will be beyond your ability to handle. When that happens, you're going to have to let me go forward and slay the dragons without any help from you. You understand that, don't you?"

Lena's brows contracted. "What do you mean?"

"I mean that when we get to confront the leaders of the men who kidnapped you and Adara, they may have powers and abilities that rival yours." I considered it a moment, "And anything God can do through me."

"But God can do anything!"

"Yes. He can. I can't. I'm just helping Him. I may not be able to act fast enough. If they see you helping, like you have been, you're going to be caught in the crossfire. You have to let me slay the monsters, Lena."

Lena's face flickered through so many emotions, it was clear she didn't know what to feel.

"Okay," she pouted.

I nodded. "Good."

Lena put a hand out on mind, touching the Soul Ring. "Hussar. What is this?"

I turned my hand palm up. The ring had stopped glowing. "This is a weapon. It takes sin and evil, and absorbs it as a weapon. But it can also take virtue and prayer and make that a weapon... at least, I think so. We have not tested that part out yet."

Lena cocked her head to one side. "Why haven't you?"

"Anyone I could test it on have been people I could fight myself. And since we haven't tested this out yet, the last thing we want is to try it out and it blows up on me." I raised my hand, palm facing me, and bent my ring finger down. "I don't want to be known as Frodo if I can avoid it."

Lena laughed. She stopped laughing. Her head whipped around to one side. "He knows!"

Lena dropped to the floor from the chair and raced to the door. She ripped it open. There was a uniformed officer in the hallway. She stabbed her index finger at one of them and said, "You know!"

The cop looked very confused.

If you want to see a cop angry, it's easy.

1) Show a cop someone who has committed crimes against women and/or children.

2) Show a cop a cop killer.

3) Worst of all, show a cop a fellow officer who was 1 or 2.

When Lena had pointed out uniformed officer Herman Horn, we had no idea that he was going to show us #3... in spades.

Horn had been a uniformed cop for over a decade. For that entire time, he had worked Potsdam. He had walked the same beat for that entire time. Occasionally, he would be allowed to drive.

Eight years ago was the first time. He had broken up a group of young Turks who had accosted a young woman. The woman had her clothes torn off. The men were on drugs and out of control. The woman said that she had been kidnapped by the men. The Turks said that they had been merely horsing around with the girl-friend of one of their number. No harm, no foul. Horn, in good cop fashion, arrested everyone and brought them in on drug use, for a start. The woman was not cuffed.

Within the hour, every man had been released from the

station. Horn had been smacked on the wrist for being "culturally insensitive" and "borderline racist."

The woman is now known as "Mrs. Horn."

Horn hadn't witnessed a similar incident until the next year, when a young girl pounded against the window of a taxi cab, screaming for help. Horn had stepped in front of the cab until the driver tried to run him over. Horn leaped onto the hood of the car, and eventually forced the driver to stop by blocking the windshield with his own body. The girl said that the driver had taken her past her stop miles back and had kidnapped her. The driver told Horn's superiors that he misunderstood, his German was no good.

Horn had been written up that time.

Only a few weeks later, things became worse. A struggling woman had been hefted by a collection of men who tried to load her into the back of a truck. Horn came in swinging with his baton. Reading the report of witnesses and even reviewing the video tape, Horn was an action hero.

There began a refrain that Horn would hear constantly over the course of the next few years. The woman was lying. The woman was drunk. The woman was a whore. Horn was a racist. Horn assumed bad intention. Horn needed to be retrained.

This last slander was slapped on Horn by one of the local Imams. The Imam threatened retaliation against the "racist *politzei*." There would be riots! There would be blood! There would be justice!

This was the nail in Horn's coffin. Since then, every time he was up for a promotion, Horn had been stymied. He passed the equivalent of the sergeant's exam and had surpassed other officers who had been promoted over him. He had applied to be Kommissar, but Horn would be rejected and refused any attempt to become promoted.

No matter who Horn talked to, he would always be shot down

and told to sit down and shut up. Their internal affairs department ignored him. Superiors always slapped him down. Fellow cops grumbled, but what could they do?

Instead, Horn had been ordered to arrest fathers who claimed their daughters had been stolen. The fathers were making racist assumptions about poor immigrant refugees.

The man who had scuttled Horn's political career was, much to my anticipation, was newly-minted Imam Kozbar—the man who had tried to kill me repeatedly in London.

Even dead, this son of a bitch is a hemorrhoid. How much human wreckage has he left strewn behind him?

By the time we were done with the interrogation, Berger wasn't smiling so much as he was baring teeth.

While every available police officer charged down to have a long conversation with Horn's superiors, I took out my cell phone and texted Rabbi Weil. I tapped out the text, showed it to Lena, and she confirmed that I was going to send what I thought I typed.

I told him it was almost time to move.

As the cops rushed out, Pearson drifted over to me. I had been placed in a desk chair and parked, while Horn had been interrogated. Pearson sat on the desk top and leaned over to me. "Do you think that we can let the *politzei* try to take this group?"

I frowned and looked around. Lena was the only other person who could hear. Adara was asleep, and all the cops were ignoring me now that they had a target to come down on.

I said quietly, "No idea. Depends on what they have, really. Let's face it, if this place is where Jayden has been hiding, that's one thing. I think the *poltizei* can chase her off. Shooting her is like slapping her. If half the Potsdam tactical team fill her with lead, she'll buzz off. But you heard what Gaiman said. A legion of demons? And when there are enough demons, they whip out Asmodeus?" I shook my head. "It's going to be a bloodbath. And we have to move sooner rather than later. Tonight, if we can."

Pearson's eyebrows went up. "Impatient, aren't we?"

I shook my head. "We've been dismantling their network, piece by piece. If Jayden has even a shred of brains in her head, she'll try to speed up the process and raise as many demons as she can as soon as she can. Gaiman said that this place has equipment the Nazis were going to use to raise a demon, so she should be fully equipped. But that description has gotta be something we can use."

Pearson nodded and wandered away without another word. I tracked him, but my neck hurt to turn it that much. I watched him go over to Officer Horn. After a quick exchange, Pearson patted him on the arm and came straight back to me.

"How are you doing?" Pearson asked. "Because I have a location. We can move on it, but only if you're certain that you can get there and be ready to get shot at again."

I smiled at him. I figured that God would give me everything I needed, assuming He hadn't already. Between the Soul Ring and my two backup plans, Pearson and I might have been ready to go to war.

"I need to contact two people," I told him. "As soon as I have a location."

Pearson's eyes narrowed, as though he didn't trust me. "Who do you know around here? I've been with you every step of the way."

My smile flicked a little wider. "Exactly."

Pearson's head tilted. "What are you up to?"

"Aside from my first excursion against an entire prison riot, I endeavor not to tackle anyone or anything alone. I had backup against the cult. I called in the Feds against the mayor. In London, I had you. Trust me on this."

Pearson sighed. "It's a place called Groß Glienicke."

"Where the bleep is that?" I asked.

Pearson smiled. "Let's show you."

I held up a hand and looked to Lena. I forced myself to bend over close to her. Lena stepped forward and pushed me back so she could come to me, and I wouldn't have to bend.

"Are you going now?" Lena asked me straight.

"I am."

Lena studied my face for a long moment. She looked over my bruises and my bandages. "Will you be able to fight?"

I nodded. "Always."

She sucked in her lips and chewed on them. She let them go. "Can no one else do it?"

I let myself laugh, no matter how much it hurt. "If they could, I'd let them. Trust me on that."

Lena patted me on the arm. "Then go. Kill monsters."

"Deal."

Groß Glienicke was the perfect place for an Agatha Christie murder mystery. It was a land of plains and lakes and manor houses. It stopped just short of being perfectly rural, but one could easily see where the wild flora stopped, and the perfectly trimmed and manicured homes began.

But there was only one house that Officer Horn could point to for the slavery ring to operate out of. Not only because of the crying fathers who claimed to know where their daughters had been taken; not only because the estate had been purchased and allowed to go to pot; but also because local folklore had it that, during the 1930s and 1940s, the chief of the SS, Himmler, had used it during summer months, and that freak was more into the occult than even Adolf Hitler. There had often been rumors about what went on in the manner hose, but no one dared search it then. No one wanted American GIs dissecting both the manor house and the town.

We drove up to the front gate. The iron fence was tall enough for me to wonder if they were models for Arkham Asylum or a scale model for King Kong—thirty feet tall, if they were an inch, topped with spikes.

We knew it was the place as soon as we saw it. I could smell the evil coming off of the land.

Pearson drove past the fence and parked half a mile away. "Are you sure you're up for this?"

"I have to be," I told him.

"Well, now would be a great time to pray for angels. Or healing. Or a fireball to vaporize the building."

I smiled. He remembered my incident with the mayor. "We have contingencies already, so we shouldn't need angels. I can't call down fire from the sky, there are probably still innocents trapped inside. As for healing ... let's see if the new toy works."

I made my right hand into a fist, then covered it with my left. I wasn't using Asiatic meditative poses but covering the Soul Ring with my own hand, hoping to contain a blast if anything should go horribly wrong. Since the whole Soul Stone could wreck cities, I only wanted to risk myself for the first trial run.

As noted before, I didn't want to bother the Lord God if I could help it. I preferred using what God had already given me before asking for anything else. Much had been given. Much was expected. And I had a full tool belt. Until I threw everything I had at the problem, it felt greedy to ask.

Heal, I thought at the ring.

The Soul Ring responded.

Instead of issuing forth from the jewel in the ring, the energy shot down from my arm and into me, in a rush. It didn't show externally, but my body screamed as it repaired itself. My ribs creaked as they healed. The bruise that was my body flowed back into it's original shape.

The short version—every time a chiropractor pops something back into place, there is usually a sharp pop. The sensation was one part pain, one part pleasure, and one part the sense that a puzzle piece has just been snapped back into place.

Now imagine that over the entire body, and you have a general sense of what it was like.

My eyes snapped open, and I took a deep breath, like I had been drowning.

My body shook like a wet dog. I snapped up straight.

Pearson shot back, his back against the door. He was ready to go through it. "Are you all right, or am I exorcising you, too?"

I held out my hands, bracing myself against the door. "I'm good. I'm good. Let's go."

This time, Pearson and I did our best to bring the trunk. We each had a rifle, a shotgun, a paintball gun, two handguns, and as much ammunition as we could carry. We were loaded up for war. We looked over the weapons left in the trunk. I frowned. "I really wish we could take more."

From behind us someone said, "Nice collection."

Pearson and I both turned. I had the shotgun level and ready, Pearson the paintball gun.

Kommissar Berger simply stood there, hands in his pockets. A small smile played out on the corner of his lips. "Can anyone join this party? Or is it invite only?"

"Depends. You want to play?" I asked. "Or shut us down?"

Berger rolled his eyes, reached past us both, and grabbed another shotgun, a sidearm, and went straight to stuffing magazines into his pockets. He took the trunk, slammed it down, and turned towards us. "Are you coming?"

I waved him through. "After you."

He racked the gun to feed the magazine. "*Danke.*"

As we made our way back to the manner house, Pearson asked, "What brought you out after us?"

Berger spared him a glance. "Right now, there are dozens of *politzei* tearing apart the local corruption. Once they get someone to break, it will take hours for a tactical team to get together. Even assuming that this group of Jihadi psychopaths hear nothing about their protection system falling apart, they could sacrifice dozens of women between now and the time the *politzei* get their act together."

Pearson and I exchanged a look behind Berger's back. "You think that Gaiman was telling the truth about sacrifices?"

Berger tossed a glance over his shoulder at me. "I'm certain that Gaiman believes it. It may even be that sacrifices are happening. Do I believe in actual demons? If I did, I'm not sure I could do the job. Though I have faked multiple faiths, depending on who the suspect hates the most."

We came at the manner house from the side. The woods on that end were thick, and provided plenty of cover, straight to the house itself.

But we didn't want to try for the front door. If someone didn't have that rigged with a Claymore mine, Berger, Pearson and I would all be surprised. I helped Berger up to the window on the side of the house. He had no problem with opening the widow and sliding in. He reached out and helped us in.

The first room looked like a small den. Bookcases went clear to the ceiling. There was an office desk up against the windows. My shotgun was up and ready.

I cautiously slid up to the door and pressed my ear against it. There were no sounds. I cracked the door open. No one to the right of it. I swung the door open, cleared right, then swung left.

There were six armed men casually walking down the brightly lit hallway, chatting amicably. Their fezzes were marked with the Swastika, but the rest of their clothing was casual.

Boom went my shotgun. The first two went down without even realizing what happened. I racked and fired again. *Ch-ch,boom.* I stepped out of the door, charging into them. *Ch-ch,boom. Ch-ch,boom.* The last man standing barely had his hand on his sidearm when I leaped for him. Driving my elbow into his face.

Every door in the hall in front of me opened. Every man who poked his head out held a weapon.

Crap.

I put my right shoulder up against the wall opposite the den we'd entered and backpedaled, firing at any target I saw. Berger was on one knee in the doorway, firing with his sidearm. Pearson was above him, firing with the AK-47. They covered as I came back and threw myself through the den door.

"I think we're screwed," Berger said as we closed the door and dropped one of the bookcases to barricade it.

I grabbed my phone and dialed. When I heard the click, I said, "Dreidel dreidel dreidel, that I made out of clay. Dreidel dreidel dreidel, dreidel I shall play."

Berger looked at me like I had lost my mind, singing a children's tune in the middle of a shootout. I slipped the phone away and said, "Everyone, behind the desk. We'll need cover."

The door exploded with bullets ripping through it. They kicked open part of the door. Then they shot through the bookcase we dropped in front of it.

The three of us returned fire, into the doorway and just on either side of it. Pearson and I used the AK rifles. Berger used the shotgun from time to time, wanting a better shot than just blindly firing into the hall.

A grenade rolled into the den.

"Grenade!" Berger called.

The windows to the side of the den blew in as a shape crashed through. It was long-limbed and spindly. It was built along the line of a department store mannequin but fast and mobile. It scooped up the grenade and spun in one motion, throwing it into the hallway. It exploded, scattering the men outside. Fresh men came in moments later, and smacked right into the shape.

It grabbed a gun and bent the barrel back, one-handed. Ripping the gun away, it punched into the man's throat at the same time. It took the gun and threw it so hard, it embedded itself in another terrorist's face.

Ch-ch.

It shot forward and deflected the gun with one hand as it spun backwards, the heel of its foot kicking the Jihadi off of his feet.

It came to its feet, grabbed a terrorist, and drove a knee into his stomach. Without resetting the foot, it mule-kicked into an approaching gunman, kicking the gun away. It whirled and hurled the gunman aside, sending him crashing into his backup.

Berger watched the whirlwind of chaos and destruction. "What the *fuck* was that?"

It was why angels had not clamored to our side. God had granted me either a little foresight or a lot of luck. It only occurred to me when I met Adara's grandfather—a Rabbi of Prague. He had the key to an ancient secret.

Back in the hospital room in Prague I had said one word to Adara's grandfather, Rabbi Weil. He nodded, and I told Lena to tell him how many we needed. "As many as possible."

That word harkened back to a mythology in Jewish folklore. It referred to a protector of the Jewish Ghetto specific to Prague.

It was what I said to Berger right now.

That word was "Golem."

21 / ATTACK OF THE OVEN-BAKED GOLEM

The oldest stories of golems date to early Judaism. Like the biblical Adam, all golems are created from mud by those close to divinity, but no golem made by man was supposed to be fully human. It was traditionally made from clay and activated via the use of Hebrew letters forming one of the Names of God—this would be written on a piece of paper and inserted in the golem's mouth or forehead. One of the more common versions, the Golem of Prague, the Hebrew word *emet* ("truth") was written on its forehead—removing one letter made it "death," deactivating the golem.

Tradition had it that the golem was the defender of the Jewish people, going back to the 1200s.

And as I watched one buzz-saw through the Jihadis, I wondered how anything could stop it.

"What do you mean golem?" Berger whispered harshly, his shotgun on the golem.

I reached over and gently deflected his muzzle. "Don't shoot him. You'll just make him mad." I whispered. "The little girl we have with us?" I asked over my shotgun. "Tiny brunette? Her grandfather is the Rabbi of Prague. Her parents are in construction."

Berger looked at me like I was insane. "You're serious."

"Yes. Her father managed it all by phone. They got molds for clothing mannequins, poured in mud, and carved a gash for a mouth so the holy scriptures could be slid in."

Berger looked at the golem. "It's too solid to be clay."

"They were fired clay. I don't know where. Rabbi Weil just told me it was ..." I pulled out my phone, didn't even try to pronounce the word, and handed it to Berger. "That."

Berger read the text. He laughed and choked at the same time. "Sachsenhausen! They fired it at Sachsenhausen!"

"What is it? A pizza place? That's the only place I can think of that would have an oven big enough."

"It's a concentration camp! It's a museum now, but it's a concentration camp!"

I blinked. *Well, they have ovens big enough for the job. I'm surprised they still work, though.* "Right." I grabbed my phone back. I looked to the golem. It had dropped the last gunman. "Lead the way to the ritual."

The golem nodded and moved forward. I raced after him. "Don't dawdle, guys, run!"

The golem charged ahead, smashing through Nazi Muslims trying to raise demons. *Yeesh, it's just like a Hellboy comic.* "*Golem golem golem, I built him out of clay. Golem golem golem, evil we shall slay.*"

The golem didn't need much to cut through resistance in the house. Its momentum was more than enough to bowl over most anyone in the way. I ran with my shotgun up and ready. Any time there was a Jihadi smart enough to stay hidden until the golem passed, Berger and I were usually there, firing a shotgun blast when he popped into our line of sight.

We made it to the front room of the manner house. It looked like the main entrance to *Gone with the Wind*—large sweeping staircase, elegant wallpaper, red carpet from the door and up the stairs.

Then there were the Jihadis on the upper walkway.

The golem didn't even pay attention to them until they started firing. He swiveled on an ankle into a leap up the stairs, taking great galloping leaps of six at a time. Bullets clanged and clattered against it. Occasionally, a chip or two came off the golem. It didn't stop or slow. It leaped for the top of the banister and swung around it like the blade of a blender, kicked one Jihadi off the walkway, swung around, and threw itself into the next one in sequence. The golem launched itself like a missile, feet first, knocking one gunman off his feet, and slamming the next one against the wall.

Without time for gravity to take effect, the golem bent its knees with the impact and pushed off, launching at the remaining gunman. He crashed into the gunman with his shoulder. The golem and the gunman went down in a crash. The golem rolled down the walkway, a clay ball that smashed through the legs of another shooter. It launched from the walkway and clothes-lined two of the last gunmen.

The final shooter blasted the golem full in the chest with his AK-47. The chest plate formed cracks and dents, spider-webbing across the golem's body. Except for some chips, the golem stayed together. None of the bullets even penetrated.

The golem grabbed the gunmen and threw both of them off the walkway. The golem used the Jihadi as a landing pad, leaving a smear in the marble floor.

The golem rose as though it had done nothing interesting and sprinted away, the three of us trailing behind.

If everything could be this easy, Lord, I'll be perfectly happy with that. Thanks.

The golem led us straight to a wall behind the stairs. The golem didn't wait for us to figure anything but immediately clawed at the wood paneling, ripping away the false front. Berger had to step back to avoid flying wood chips and panel sections, Pearson behind me. By the time the golem was finished ripping the front to pieces, it revealed a metal door in a concrete setting that looked like the top part of a bunker.

The golem moved as though it was impatient. It raised its knee and stomped on the metal door at the point where the lock met the frame. The metal around the handle and lock twisted and tore as the door flew open. From the staircase came the ugly, hideous odor of death, putrefaction, and evil on top of it, each horrid smell fighting the other for dominance in my brain.

The golem had led the way to the ritual and would have probably stopped there, if the guards at the bottom of the stairs hadn't opened fire. It casually, smoothly, almost elegantly, swan dived from the top of the concrete steps and "landed" with its hands in the throats of both gunmen. They slammed against the bunker wall, supporting the weight of the golem with the fragile bones in their necks. The golem's feet touched the landing and hurled both bodies down the staircase. It charged down the stairs.

I grabbed Berger by the shoulder but stared into the darkness ahead of us. "Stay here."

Berger gave me a look that doubted my mental health. "*Vas?* You want to keep me back here?"

I nodded without looking at him. The golem continued to crash and smash down the staircase. The occasional scream and gunshot drifted up to us. They got further and further with each passing second. "We don't want to be bottle necked up here. If we need to bug out in short order, we don't want to run into men throwing grenades down the stairs."

It was perfectly truthful... but not all of the truth. I didn't tell him one of the other, darker reasons I needed *him* up there. None of us knew for certain who would be down there, or how many—or worse, *what*—but Pearson and I at least had an idea. The last thing we needed was Berger running into demonic forces face to face.

Bad enough he had to wrap his brain around a golem running point for us in the middle of a gunfight. At this minute, he didn't need to be confronted by all the powers of Hell. If there was a later, Pearson and I could explain the facts of the afterlife to him.

Berger nodded and took up a sentry position, shotgun ready. I looked to Pearson and nodded, and the two of us went into the abyss below. We followed the trail of casings, bullets and bodies. There were lamps at every landing, providing enough light for us to see without needing sonar.

And we're all glad that its on our side, aren't we?

Pearson and I ran down several stories into the Earth. My in-depth knowledge of World War Two trivia was ephemeral on a good day, but I recalled once hearing that the Nazis had spent much of the latter parts of the war moving much of their operation underground. I hadn't known just how deep some of these things had gotten.

Then again, when the average bombing run drops by the ton, deeper is better.

We made it to the bottom of the stairs, and stopped just short of running into the golem. It stood at the bottom of the stairs, motionless. It had been given its orders, and it had followed them perfectly.

We were in the middle of the ceremony to raise demons.

The stairs emptied out into a wide concrete hall. The floor looked like a Mosque during prayers. Row upon row of kneeling, bowing Jihadis lined the floor, each on a rug, and each rug had an AK-47 to one side. Each of the prayerful had the same fez with Swastika on it that we had first encountered at Morderberg.

The opposite end of the room had a raised platform. Off to the side was a small, neat little man in a suit and tie, standing in front of a statue of ... some monster that looked like HP Lovecraft tried to design a dragon. The Swastika behind the platform was partially obscured by an altar of black marble, with a woman's naked form strapped down and on display. She had been raped and vivisected. Her heart was in the upraised hand of Jayden the succubus. Jayden was again, still, nude—unless one counted treating blood like body paint as being "covered."

The succubus was in the middle of a gleeful roar as we entered. She laughed in triumph, both hands elevating the heart like it was a Host at Communion.

Jayden's face snapped towards us. Instead of anger, she grinned broadly. "You're too late, *saint*," she spat. "*Priest*. You're far too late. You should have been here half an hour ago." Jayden dropped the heart back into the woman's body. "You may be glad that you rushed us. That you deprived us of sacrifice. That we must begin at the depths of our powers instead of the highest. But I guarantee that you will not live long enough to gloat about it."

The men at prayer on the floor looked up and around, trying to find who Jayden was talking to.

"*Nien*," she roared. "Let them be the first *living* sacrifices to our lord!" She swung a bloody hand to point at the ugly statue on stage, behind the man in the suit. "Asmodeus!"

The Jihadis pushed to their feet and fell back from the center of the room, giving us plenty of room to fire at Jayden and giving the golem a clear running field for her.

Jayden stepped back from the altar, and the altar fell into the platform, as though the center of the stage had collapsed in on itself. A sudden breeze wafted out, adding to the smell of evil in the room. It hit me like a truck, rocking me back.

But we're underground. Did someone open a window, or...

From the hole in the stage, a pillar of fire roared to life, punching through the concrete ceiling. A red, clawed hand reached out from the fire and grabbed the stage, igniting it as the creature hauled itself out from the depths of Hell.

I dropped the shotgun to dangle from my shoulder and swept up the AK-47. Without any hesitation, I opened fire on the

Jihadis. They had been content to just stay out of the way while the pillar of fire opened up. I swept it back and forth as I fell back into the concrete doorway. Bullets bounced all around me. But they ricocheted off of the concrete cover, striking fellow gunmen.

Father Pearson opened fire with his holy water paintball gun, firing for Jayden. The succubus fell back, laughing—but she didn't dare come closer, into Pearson's range.

The golem didn't need orders. It sprang forward, darting for the stage. It leaped for Jayden.

The thing from the pit leaped from the pillar of fire. It was red, covered in scales. The spaces between the scales were lines of fire up and down its body. The head ... like a goat covered in scales, with wolf teeth. It was rippling with muscles that made steroids seem pale in comparison. Its eyes glowed an icy blue, and the ram horns came to spear tips.

When the demon rammed into the golem, the golem came to a standstill. The golem and the demon grabbed each other like wrestlers. The golem's legs tucked under itself and kicked the demon in the face. Its head rocked back only a little, but the golem grabbed the ram's horns and twisted, breaking its neck. The golem found its feet. The golem's upper torso spun around, taking the demon's corpse with it. Golem hurled it into the pillar of fire like garbage.

Then three more demons leaped forward, piling on the golem. The golem fought back, even with its arms pinned. The legs freely kicked out, striking the back of heads, knees, hips, shoulders.

But the demons held fast.

And then other claws came forth from the pillar of fire.

The golem's head turned a full 180 degrees and looked at us. It screamed, "*Run!*"

We ran.

We pounded our way up the stairs, charging up the barely lit concrete steps. I smashed every other lamp as I ran past. If we were going to have the host of Hell on our heels, they could find their way up in the dark.

We made it up three sets of staircases when the growls and the roaring began. The darkness behind us was filled with an eerie red glow. The snarling sounded like a pack of hungry junkyard dogs. A hot breeze followed after us, with the sound of a roaring fire closing in on us.

When I saw the bright light from up ahead, I screamed out, "Berger! Run!"

We came up the last stairs. Berger was already moving. Pearson and I came out and wheeled around the doorway for the front door.

The front door, as I thought, was wired with explosives. I fired at it with the rifle, causing the booby trap to explode, ripping the door from its hinges. The three of us charged through the front door. The massive staircase in the main room exploded, filling the room with fire and ripped through the next three stories of the manner house, then the ceiling.

I grabbed a Bluetooth earpiece and turned it on, jamming it in my ear.

Berger looked at me and slowed down a little so he could call out over the roaring fires, "Did you hit a gas main?"

I shook my head at him. I held up a hand to stop the run. I turned around to the fiery wreck that was the house and swapped out to the shotgun. I ejected the buckshot and replaced it with a rotation of holy salt and dragon's breath. The center section of the manor house was a massive fire ball. The back of the house had a massive pillar of fire shooting straight to the sky.

"No," I answered, racking the slide to eject the last of the buckshot from the chamber. "Not the gas main."

The remaining windows of the house exploded as winged abominations flew out, roaring and covered in fire. More demons roared out of the pillar of fire. A trio of them came out together, carrying the golem with them. They flew off in three different directions, ripping the golem apart and scattering its limbs.

The Bluetooth said, "Bluetooth on. BEEP. Connected."

I said into the earpiece, "Then the winged hussars arrived."

Berger looked at me like I had lost my mind and proceeded to fire into the demons, making like they were skeet.

The demons he struck saw Berger and raced for him.

Pearson and I dropped to one knee and waited for the demons.

The demons flew closerto us.

We held our fire.

Their razor-sharp wolf teeth dripped with acid and snarled with rage.

Pearson and I did nothing. Berger fired frantically, to no effect.

They were ravenous demons with muscles the size of my thigh, practically bathed in napalm. They held no fear.

The Earth shook with the force of a minor earthquake. Heavy footsteps of unstoppable beings stampeded towards us. Nothing would stop them. Nothing could stop them as they charged from behind.

The demons were just within our range when Pearson and I both blasted them with holy water, holy salt, and fire. The demons flinched and recoiled, stopping in the air within rock-throwing distance of our position.

Then our backup arrived.

The army of golems leaped over our heads and slammed into the demonic forces, pummeling them with fists of clay. Demons fell from the sky as golems ripped the wings off them. Wolf jaws in goat faces clamped down on clay arms, and the golems responded with grabbing the jaws and ripping them open. The demons may have been from Hell itself, but the golems were animated by the word of God Himself.

As I told Pearson when we knew where we were going, I had to make two phone calls. The first was to Adara's grandfather, the Rabbi of Prague. We both knew the story of the golem. In myth, it was a one of a kind creature. Only one was needed to face the threats and horrors faced by the community.

But that was before the dawn of mass production and construction companies.

I grabbed one of Berger's arms, and Pearson grabbed the other one, half-leading half-dragging him off to the bushes and flora to the side. More demons emerged from the fires and screamed as they swooped in for us. More golems leaped from the cover of bushes and crashed into the demons.

Then the bushes erupted with gunfire as the Polish special forces unleashed the full force of their weapons. All of them carried what looked like black AK-47s, but were actually Saiga 366s—fully automatic shotguns. They were armed full of shells loaded with holy salt, spraying the demons at point-blank range. Other Polish commandos were armed with paintball guns, the balls themselves filled with holy water.

Further back in the woods were Polish priests, chanting and praying the rite of exorcism.

They had been my second phone call. Pearson had told me that Western Europe had largely stopped believing in exorcism and the supernatural. Poland is very proud to *not* be Western Europe. When I invited them over for an illegal operation to shoot up Nazi-raised demons in Germany, they apparently had a lot of people who were up for "covert entry and live fire exercises."

The activation phrase for both them and the golems was *Then the winged Hussars arrived.* Apparently, Sabaton was very popular in Poland, especially among those with a certain set of skills.

Pearson and I got Berger into the care of the Polish gunmen. Pearson got into position and started chanting his own prayers as he fired into the demons.

I turned back to the demons and clenched and unclenched my fists. I looked over the battlefield of flailing demons pelted with holiness, and golems exchanging blows with demons that rocked the earth.

There was just one person missing from the festivities.

"Jayden!" I bellowed. "Come on out, you cowardly whore from Hell!"

A demon flew in front of me, and I casually blasted it with holy salt. I jammed the muzzle at the wolf fangs and fired again, filling the mouth with fire. It reared back, surprised, but then I racked it and fired more salt into its eyes. It roared and howled, falling back.

I walked past it, grabbing a Mass card from my back pocket. I jammed it into the demon's mouth, and it gagged, falling back some more.

A demon roared to my left, disengaging from the line of golems. A fresh demon swooped in to engage the golem as the other one went for the easy prey—me.

I didn't waste any time. It flew for me. I reached behind me and grabbed a pocket full of holy salt and hurled it into the demon's face. It cried out like an injured goat and fell back. I fired as fast as I could with the shotgun. *Ch-ch, boom. Ch-ch, boom. Ch-ch, boom. Ch-ch, boom.*

Between the holy salt and the dragon's breath, it had reduced the demon's head to mush, leaving a quickly deflating body at one end, and the Swastika-covered fez on top.

A fez. Wait a second—

I looked around. Every other demon wore a fez, just like the Jihadists back in the concrete bunker. Meaning that some of the demons were just that—manifest demons. If Jayden's rant was to be believed before the portal to Hell opened up, these were just the lesser demons. Some of the others had latched onto a Jihadi gunman.

At least, we know hat happened to them.

I waded into the battlefield and kept up the pressure, cutting a swath into the demons with my shotgun. When I ran out of ammo in the shotgun, the demons started coming fast and furious. I switched to the paintball gun and fired it on full automatic, spraying holy water pellets left and right like I was working a scythe and mowing down rows of corn instead of rows of demons. Spraying them with holy water grounded them—their wings couldn't carry them anymore. This put them on the same plane, and only so many could charge me at once before they stumbled over each other. The constant stream of water sawed through them, cutting the demons in half.

Then I ran out of pellets in the gun, leaving the fully-healthy demons charging for me—and no time for me to reload.

I was ready for them. Mass cards drove them back and burned them when I tossed them into the face of a demon. Holy water sprays from an atomizer worked at short range, weakening them. When those ran out, I grabbed a plastic package of holy oil and slapped it against my knuckles, breaking the package.

Holy oil knuckles really help when punching demons in the face. And everywhere else.

After the last of the holy oil burned off my knuckles, I reached into my back pocket, threaded my fingers through the strands of a rosary and roundhouse-punched the next demon with the rosary beads digging into my skin and burning away its face. I back-handed it to boot, smacking it away.

Jayden dropped down behind me, her wings carrying her over to me. She grabbed my wrist and smacked the rosary beads from my fingers. She whirled me around and smiled, her sharp teeth making her look like a cat that had found a mouse to torture.

"Now that you're all out of holy weapons—" She smacked me across the face and sent me flying. I landed and rolled, hitting the ground hard. I got to my hands and feet, and she swooped in.

Jayden drove her fist in for my head. I rolled to the side, and she drove her fist a foot into the ground. She scoffed and swiped her hand out of the ground, hurling pounds of earth at me. I blocked it with my arm. She leaped in with her claws outstretched and reaching for me. I grabbed her by the wrists and fell back, flipping her over me. I rolled to my feet and faced her. She hadn't gone flying but used her wings to halt her momentum.

It was then that I realized that Jayden had waited me out. She let demons burn through my resources, then closed on me before I could reload my weapons. I was out of holy salt, water, Mass cards, and I had a few rosaries left—if I could get to them in time to use them. Jayden's first move was to throw me. She had hurled me far and away from the lines of golems and Polish commandos. I spared the battlefield a quick look. The number of golems was starting to shrink, and the demons were still coming from the house.

"Time to die, my little saint," Jayden purred.

Jayden shot in so fast, she was a blur. Her right fist crashed into the left side of my ribcage like I had been hit by a car. I growled in pain and clamped my left arm down on hers, wrapping my arm around hers to lock her into place. With a scream of mostly pain, I punched her in the face with my right. She grabbed my wrist before I made contact.

Jayden smiled at me. "My powers only grow as the portal to home stays open, *saint*."

I growled through gritted teeth, trying not to scream in pain. I reared back and rammed my forehead into her perfect pert nose. "I —" And again. "—am not—" And once more. "—a saint!"

Jayen's head rocked back a little; she staggered slightly, but she quickly retained her footing. "Not yet."

Jayden head butted me in the sternum and *cracked* it. She did it again, only this time striking my collar bone with her forehead, snapping it out of place. And again.

I screamed in pain, unable to hold pressure on either of my arms.

Jayden smirked and shoved me back with a flick of her fingers. I had to gasp for breath as the collar bone pressed in on my airways.

"No," she said, making even that sound lascivious. "You're not a saint yet. And by the time I'm done with you, I don't think you will be." She slapped me like a girl, knowing I couldn't stop her. She grabbed my shirt and brought me in close, as if for a kiss. "I think I'll save you for dessert, little saint. You and I can spend *hours* and *hours* getting to know each other. By the time I'm done *fucking* you to death, you won't even remember the name of your God, to hell with the name of your wife and child. I'll own you in this life, and in the next. I will suck the life out of your body through your cock, and you'll beg me not to stop."

Jayden slashed me with her poisoned claws, ripping open the skin of my chest. My blood burned the tips of her claws off, but I felt the poison burn in my veins, filling me with lust despite the pain—this made the lust even more painful.

"You'll only be the cherry on top of my reward," she boasted.

"When I have fulfilled my geas, the commands placed upon me by Kozbar, I will be free to roam the world and collect all the willing into my bed. And I get to *live*. Truly *live*. I will be free of my masters and their bidding. And I will pay Kozbar back for ever entrapping me in the first place." She shook me like a doll. "Maybe I should visit his Mosque and turn it into a den of iniquity. Sounds like fun, don't you think?"

Jayden lifted me with one hand and hurled me into a pile of broken clay pottery. I landed with a smash and clatter, my body writhing in pain and hormones. My breath was so constricted, I couldn't even scream.

Jayden turned away from me and left me for dead. She spread her great bat wings and lifted herself into the air. She flew away from the shooting gallery on the front lines, into the pillar of fire.

The pillar of fire faded back, diminishing.

Standing in its place was a dragon, ten stories tall and a wing-span the length of the house. The armored scales of its body were blood red, like the hair of the succubus who went in. The great green eyes were slit like a cat's. With a swipe of her tail, she threw half of the manor house into the garden off the side of the house—cutting off an escape route for the Poles.

The dragon ... Jayden ... was stomping her way to the Polish commandos and what was left of the dwindling golems. There was nothing that stood in her way.

The clay pile I was in rattled and shook with each step Jayden took as she made her way to the Polish SpecOps team. In fact, the ground shook more with each step. Instead of feeding out new demons, the portal fed Jayden energy. She continued to grow in massive dragon form, becoming taller and wider with each step.

Meanwhile, I was worthless, in so much agony I couldn't even writhe on the pile of broken clay. My veins were on fire. I couldn't breathe. I couldn't even lift my arms. If I concentrated, maybe I could stand. The agony became a white noise through which I could barely think. I had a vague notion that I needed to get up. I needed to keep moving. The Poles were a collection of bad-asses whose idea of a fun time was playing tag with Spetsnaz, but they couldn't take Jayden. The golems could barely take the lesser demons that had poured out from the portal to Hell, what chance had mortal men?

We didn't so much need a *deus ex machina* as we did just plain *Deus*.

I forced myself to think, and only one thing could come through. One rote prayer could punch through my agony.

Out of the depths, I have cried to Thee O Lord! Lord, hear my voice. Let Thine ears be attentive to the voice of my supplication.

If Thou, O Lord! Wilt mark iniquities: Lord, who shall stand it? For with Thee, there is mercy: and by reason of Thy law, I have waited on Thee, O Lord!

My soul hath relied on His word: my soul hath hoped in the Lord. From the morning watch even until night: let Israel hope in the Lord. For with the Lord, there is mercy; and with Him plentiful Redemption. And He will redeem Israel from all his iniquities. Eternal rest give unto them, O Lord! And let perpetual light shine upon them. May they rest in peace.

Lord, hear my prayer. And let my cry come unto Thee.

I took a slow, gasping breath as I became lightheaded. My fists clenched around a pile of the pottery pile... until I noticed that they were shaped like human fingers.

I wasn't in a pile of broken pottery.

I was in a pile of *golem* parts.

I stopped praying long enough to think, *How did this pile of golem parts happen? The demons didn't stop to pile them, did they? You don't do that with the dead until after the fight's over.*

A finger moved on a shattered hand. It creaked but still moved.

What if the golem parts piled themselves here?

I tensed my triceps and thrust my arm out to reach for it. The world went white from the agony for a long moment. The clay finger opened up, hollowing itself out. I pressed my index finger into it. The clay molded itself around my finger.

My thoughts became clearer. I looked two fingers down to the Soul Ring. I don't know where the next idea I had came from. It may have been me. It may have been the animating force of the golems. It may have been God Himself. But I focused on the Soul Ring with the one idea I had left.

The debris beneath me gave way suddenly. I was sinking into the pile of golem parts. Other pieces poured in on top of me.

I was slowly buried alive.

I controlled my breathing.

Bless, O my God! the repose I am about to take, that, renewing my strength, I may be better enabled to serve Thee. Pour down Thy blessings, O Lord! On my parents, relations, friends, and enemies. Protect the Pope, our Bishop, and all the Pastors of Thy holy Church. Assist the poor and the afflicted, and those who are now in their last agony. Look with an eye of pity on the suffering souls in purgatory, put an end to their torments, and lead them forth into everlasting joy.

As I prayed my heart out, the red dragon reared back its ugly head and darted forth, spewing fire all over the greenery. Three commandos died in an instant, consumed by white-hot flame. The other commandos formed an orderly retreat, firing for the dragon's head and body as much as they could with their dwindling supplies. The golems charged forward in a futile effort to buy the commandos more time. The dragon's tail swept them away, shattering them.

The Poles disappeared into the trees, and Jayden kicked through them, sending massive trees I was scattering across the landscape like toothpicks. A massive flap of her wings created a gale force gust of wind and threw bushes and uprooted trees.

It created a perfect pathway to the commandos and the priests they brought with them.

Only one person who wasn't running stayed behind. He didn't show his back to the dragon and didn't run. He tossed his paintball gun to one side. He discarded his empty rifle and shotgun. The only thing in his hands was his pectoral cross.

Father Michael Pearson, combat exorcist, stood and faced the dragon.

"You shall not pass, you vile serpent," Pearson called. "The only way to get to these men is through me, corrupter of souls. And you shall not pass me. For my strength is the Lord."

The dragon stared at Pearson a moment ... and rolled her eyes. She turned her attention away from Pearson a moment and spat a brief ball of fire. It landed between the commandos and their vehicles. With their path blocked, Jayden turned her serpentine attention back to Pearson.

"And what will you do to me, little man?" Jayden asked, her voice still sounding like her succubi form, seductive and X-rated, even though her form didn't support it. "Cast me back to Hell? My master's strength grows with each minute. Within the hour, Asmodeus will rise and destroy you all. You think that *this* form is the horror you have to face? No. My master will rise and lay waste to all you know and love. You will all die screaming, in horror and pain. And there is nothing that any of you can do to stop it. Your miracle worker, your petty *saint*, is broken by my hands. Right now, he burns for me and my touch. And when I am done with you, I will ruin him for Heaven, and only Hell will take him in. You have not the faith or the strength to stop the inevitable!"

Pearson smiled. "In my time, I've faced demons of all shapes and sizes and forms. Do you know what all of you blighters have in common?"

The dragon snorted, fire coming out her nose. "No. What?"

"When you gloat, you all bloody talk too much."

Jayden scoffed and reared back once more to turn Pearson, the commandos, and all of their priests to charcoal cinders.

Before she struck, a massive clay fist the size of a wrecking ball smashed into the dragon's face. Jayden's head snapped to one side. Her entire body rocked to one side, and the dragon staggered, falling backwards into trees that hadn't yet been uprooted.

Then she spotted me.

There I stood, encased in layers of animated clay as tall as the dragon. The clay wings on the back spread out, ready to strike or shield. The clay on the chest piece shifted to form a cross that was the length and width of the chest. Even though the clay mech didn't need a head, it formed one. It was in the shape of a plate-iron helmet, with two horizontal, rectangular eye slits. Animated by the power of God, the clay had healed me, repaired my body, and each fragment and pinch of dust had gathered together and formed the towering Templar form around me.

Through the head of the massive golem mech, my voice boomed. "Do you have a moment to talk about our Lord and Savior, Jesus Christ?"

The massive clay mech I controlled stepped forward and took a leap for the dragon. Its titanic clay fist held high and came down on the dragon's skull with the force of a missile strike. Jayden's head was driven down by the force of the blow. Her body spun around. Her wing swept up for the mech's head—the spiked tips on the wings threatening to spear through the clay mech.

The wing on my golem mech came up to meet the strike. The sharp tips dug in and became stuck there. I pulled back my wing, yanking the dragon into my waiting fist. The right hook on the mech swung back in a back fist that made the dragon's head go *crunch*.

Jayden wouldn't give in, though. She twisted her body, pulling the wing spears free of the clay. She reared back and spouted fire at me. The golem mech folded the wings defensively against the fire. I charged in and backhanded her with the right wing. With the left wing still folded around the mech, I charged, slamming into her. I drove a massive clay uppercut into Jayden's scaled belly. She staggered back, and made a sound like a mountain vomiting, though nothing came up. The scaly eyes locked onto me before she and leaped. Her claws came in from both sides, too close for the wings to absorb the blow. The mech blocked with both forearms. I shot the massive clay hands forward and grabbed Jayden by the shoulders.

I drove the knee of the golem right into the dragon's chest.

Jayden roared in pain, but lashed out, her mouth clamping down onto the mech's left shoulder. Since the clay didn't have nerves to damage or muscles to restrict, the arms moved just fine—both hands clamped down on the dragon's neck, just below her head. It choked off the windpipe and the source of the flame. The fire burned within her throat, making the dragon's entire neck glow with the withheld heat.

The dragon's claws came up and tore at the thumbs on her throat. It allowed her to breathe, if not necessarily breathe fire. Jayden's tail came up and swept the giant arms aside and followed with a massive claw into the side of the clay mech. The claws sank deep into the mech's body.

But the golem was put together from whole shards, individual pieces of golem, as well as clay dust that had gone into the golems themselves. The clay reformed around her claws and promptly ripped them off her fingers. Hot flame poured out from her finger-nails like blood from a wound.

Jayden went into a frenzy. She closed the wounded fist and backhanded me with it. Then following it up with a roundhouse from her left hand. The mech rocked with the blows and took a step back, but returned with a vicious left uppercut underneath her chin. I recoiled the left as I delivered a right cross to the drag-on's throat. The dragon gagged, spurting some fire. She wheeled around, the tail lashing me across the crusader helmet.

The mech reared forward and grabbed the left wing, both in the middle and where it met Jayden's back. I planted one foot in the dragon's back and pulled, ripping the wing right off and throwing it away. Flame spurted from the wound, and Jayden screeched. She whirled and backhanded me with her remaining right wing. The impact did little but to knock some dust off me.

The next prayer to come to me was just common sense.

I will go dressed and armed with the weapons of Saint George—

Jayden's left claws slashed at the mech's wrist. She succeeded in taking off some fingers. Material shifted to regrow the digits. I jabbed the fist into her snout.

So that my enemies, having feet will not reach me—

I stomped my forward right foot down onto her claws toes and ground them into the dirt.

Having hands will not trap me—

Jayden's dragon teeth clamped onto the mech's right bicep. With a thought, I reformed the clay to add a joint below the bite. The fist came up in an uppercut into her throat, then latched onto it in a death grip, even as Jayden ripped off the entire arm. The torn-away arm maintained its hold and wrapped the length of the arm around her throat. I shifted the material from the wings to form a new arm.

Having eyes will not see me—

With both hands, I shot forward and thrust sharpened thumbnails into Jayden's eyes. She roared.

Neither with thought can they cause me harm—

The hold on her head still secure, I pulled her head into the upraised knee from the golem.

Jayden cried out and spat a long stream of fire all around, blindly flailing in the hopes of touching me.

Firearms will not reach my body—

I noticed that, as Jayden used flames or took damage, her dragon form shrank. Converting energy to matter was one thing, especially if there was an endless stream of it from Hell. But what happened when she converted matter into energy for offensive weapons?

Knives and swords will break without touching my body, ropes, and chains will break without tying my body.

With a thought, I ordered the arm around Jayden's neck to become flat and sharp and tighten.

It cut Jayden's dragon head right off her body.

Jayden reformed the head, her body smaller now. She charged in and wrapped her arms around my left leg, using the claws of her left hand to rip through the thigh, and tossed the limb to one side. I regrew the limb, forcing my golem mech to shrink. She was also fast to learn the rules of this game, and it was a race to see who would win.

Jesus Christ protects and defends me with the power of His Holy and Divine Grace.

I drove my right fist into the back of the dragon's head, then stomped on it. Jayden detached her own head, regrew one, and slashed, taking another leg.

The Virgin of Nazareth covers me with her sacred and divine mantle, protecting me in all my dolors and afflictions.

Instead of regrowing the leg, I fell on Jayen's back. My right leg wrapped around her throat as my hands ripped the wing from her body and tossed it aside. Her tail whipped around to choke me, but she forgot that the golem mech didn't need to breathe.

And God, with His Divine Mercy and great power, is my defender against the evils and persecutions of my enemies.

I shifted the clay in my hands to become like blades. I grabbed the base of her tail and closed in, slamming both blades to meet in her flesh. The fire that poured from the wound burned the hands off and scorched the face plate.

Glorious Saint George, in the name of God, extend to me your shield and your powerful arms, defending me with your strength and your greatness—

I kneed Jayden in the spine, and I heard a *crack.* She roared and rolled us both over, flattening trees, paths, fences, fountains, and statues as we pummeled one another.

And may my enemies underneath your feet become humble and submissive to you.

I punched her in the throat.

So Be it in the Power of God—

She clawed my mech's face off.

—of Jesus Christ and of the Divine Holy Spirit.

I ripped her arm off and clubbed her with it.

Amen.

I found myself grabbing naked flesh with my own hands and threw Jayden off me. She staggered away in her succubus form, bat wings smaller than before.

I was mobile but unsteady on my feet. The clay of the golems once more reformed around me, the armor light but strong. Gauntlets formed over my fists. A helmet formed around my skull. My entire body felt invigorated. The golem clay had reformed into divine powered armor.

I suddenly had a quick image of Robert Downey, Junior saying *I! Am! Golem Man!,* followed by a Black Sabbath guitar riff, but I pushed it away.

I launched myself at Jayden, my fist driving her back, staggering. Her hands ignited with unholy black flame. I shot in, grabbed her wrist, and wrenched it into her own face. She screamed horribly before she put out the fire.

Jayden kicked off me and launched into flight, back towards the house.

She's going back to the pit. If she gets the pillar of fire started again, and recharges, then we have to do this all over again.

I readied myself to sprint after her, then paused. There was a deliberate gap in the gauntlet. On the finger of my right hand, the Soul Ring was opened and exposed.

It's a weapon, I thought. It had done in the corrupt London cop who tried to kill me, as well as the two British bigwigs who had tried to destroy London.

I pointed my fist at Jayden's back and thought about a laser putting a hole through her wing.

The Soul Ring leaped to action. The jewel glowed white for an instant before firing off a quick line of energy, like a *Star Wars* blaster.

It cut right through Jayden's wing. She screamed in pain, then in fear as the ground raced for her. She hit with a wet *thump*. She unsteadily rolled to her feet and ran for the mansion.

Screw it, I thought. *We can catch her.*

I was already off at a run before my next thought was *Who's We?*

I was only a few feet behind Jayden as she made a running leap from the front steps of the manor house and into the hole where the main staircase used to be in the front room.

I reached the same stairs and made the same leap.

Much to my surprise, with the power of the clay armor, I all but flew from the bottom front step into the hole where the concrete stairs used to be.

Jayden was only ten feet ahead of me and running for the portal.

Without thinking, I fired the Soul Ring from the hip. I put a hole in Jayden's right hip. She screamed and fell to the floor. She held the wound with her right hand. With her left, she reached out to crawl towards the raised platform, which, much to my surprise, was still there.

Also to my surprise was the neat little man in the neat little suit, standing on the platform by the statue of Asmodeus.

"Don't bother, Jayden," he said calmly. "He's got you."

Jayden cried out on pain and fear. "No! *No!*"

I stepped forward casually and calmly. Normally, I would consider arresting a perp in her condition. But there would be no way to stop her by human means. I reached down and took her arm. "Let me help you up."

Jayden looked at me in startled confusion. So did the man on the platform. She took my hand, and I raised her to her feet. I grabbed her by both shoulders and carried her so her naked behind could sit on the edge of the platform. My clay-covered hands locked to her wrists as effectively as any handcuffs.

"The way I see it," I told her, "we have two options. We talk to the Vatican, and we keep you in the secret archives next to the Ark of the Covenant—"

"That's at the bottom of the Mediterranean," the man in the suit corrected me.

I gave him a look. He merely shrugged and waited for me to continue. "Or, you get sent back."

Jayden smirked at me and spat in my face mask. "To Hell with you, *saint*. I would rather spend my last days of existence in the darkest, foulest corners of Hell then let you try to exercise *mercy* with me."

The man in the suit calmly interjected, "Which is exactly what awaits her."

"I spit on you and all your kind. You! You who were allowed a choice. To serve or to rule. We get to serve, or we are damned. *Damn* you for your mercy. Damn you for your *freedom*. Damn you for—"

I punched my right fist in her chest and fired the Soul Ring into where her heart should have been. I left a hole big enough to put my arm through. Jayden's mouth hung open, her eyes wide in shock. She struggled for breath, but couldn't draw in any.

"Go home," I said gently, then let go of her wrists.

Jayden slowly slumped back into the hole she created, and fell into the abyss.

Without Jayden as the conduit, the concrete platform rebuilt from the edges, kaleidoscoping shut.

There was the gentle sound of applause off to the side. The man in the suit clapped his delicate hands together. "Very well done, she didn't even see it coming."

I gave him a look and was about to ask him who he was and why he was still unscathed... but then I saw that he was within two circles. One of them was of chalk. The other of them was of salt.

The circles went around both him and the statue of Asmodeus.

I looked at him and took a step back.

"Yes. That's right. They summoned me a few months ago and had no problem just leaving me here to consult."

"I thought she said that Asmodeus was going to rise within the hour."

The demon Asmodeus shrugged. "She was less literal. I'm not physical yet, Detective Nolan. I'm just ... here."

From behind me, a voice called down, "Tommy! Are you all right?"

I called over my shoulder, "Right here, Pearson. But I think you're needed down here. We have to get rid of—"

Asmodeus raised his hand. "Ah ah ah! Wait. You can use me, you know. I know things. I know many things. I know who your cult served. I know what's coming next."

I arched my brows behind the clay face mask. "You want me to trust a demon?"

Asmodeus smiled. "Okay, a sample. What if I told you that Islam was started by Mohamed in a deal with a demon? A deal that would guarantee that Mohamed's name would live on forever as one of the greatest warlords of all time?"

I rolled my eyes. "I would say that it doesn't matter. That if that meant anything, we would be at constant war with a billion people on the planet until we simply nuked all of them. Considering how many converts to Christianity we've been getting, I'm thinking that any such deal—assuming it happened—is irrelevant.

It is useless data. It leads to no useful course of action. I could never prove it, except with your word, and let's be honest, Asmodeus—"

"Call me Mister Day," he said.

"Do you swear to tell the truth, the whole truth, and nothing but the truth, so help you God?"

Asmodeus flinched and fell back. "Damn you!"

I shrugged. "Not today."

Pearson touched concrete behind me. "Well well well, who do we have here? Two circles? Someone's been a naughty boy."

I smiled at Asmodeus. "Father Pearson, I'd like to introduce you to Asmodeus. He prefers to be called Mister Day. Kindly send him to Hell, would you?"

I turned from Asmodeus and walked away. He called at my back, slamming his fist against the circle like the gong from Hell. The clang reverberated throughout the room. The clay slapped down over my ears to protect me from the noise. Asmodeus boomed with a voice meant to contend with the Superbowl. "You think this is over, saint? It's not! The worst is coming for you. HP Lovecraft would have loved what's coming to get you. Do you hear me, Patron Saint of Detectives? Do you!"

I had already stopped listening.

I walked out of the basement via the concrete stairs. I was a little surprised that they were still there when everything around them was gone. Little of the main house remained either. The golem armor slid away, underneath my regular clothing.

Six of the Polish commandos were over the stairs, securing the area. The Captain saw me and waved me forward. I followed him into the front lawn, which looked like the after party at Verdun.

Sitting on one of the few benches still intact, was Kommissar Berger. He sat there, eyes wide and unseeing. I feared that he was dead for a moment, but he took a slow, deep breath.

He said that he couldn't do his job if he thought demons were real. I guess he was right. I stopped in front of him and waved my hand in front of his eyes. "Kommissar?" I prompted.

Berger's eyes flickered at me. "Was that real?"

I paused and frowned, contemplating the answer that would be better for Berger. "Which will help more?"

Berger's eyes focused on me a moment. He scoffed. "There's something that will help?"

I shrugged. "I find church helps."

Berger sighed. "I haven't been to church in a few months. Maybe it's time for a change."

"Confession first. Trust me, it makes going to mass even more effective."

He gave a humorless chuckle. "You do this often?"

"A few times. Here and there."

"And that is how you get on with your life? Church?"

"Better than booze. Or so my partner tells me. I think most of his time is spent developing new pocket explosives from whatever he can make up in his bathtub." I clapped him on the shoulder. "Look, we've got a troop of Polish commandos and a combat priest who just went through the same exact thing. I think it's time for you to start hanging out with them, and see what works. What's the worst that can happen? Church?"

Berger nodded slowly. "And what for you now, Detective Nolan? Do you just go home?"

I smiled. "Not just yet. We have some paperwork first, and then we have some debriefing to do."

I left a message with the Poles that I would meet Father Pearson at the *politizei*. The SpecOps guys said they would give Pearson a lift. They would have let Berger drive him, but they didn't trust him to drive.

I managed to make my way back to the police station. Lena and Adara were on a couch in Berger's office.

I sat down next to the couch in the armchair. I sagged into the chair and closed my eyes.

"Hussar?"

My eyes snapped open.

It was daylight.

Pearson was in the office.

Lena was next to me, grabbing my arm. Adara was just walking up on the couch.

I blinked. "Everything okay?"

Pearson nodded. "Berger is safe at home. Rabbi Weil has sent us a message. He's out of the hospital and will be picking up Adara today."

I nodded. "We need to talk with him about the golems."

Lena frowned. "Can I go with Adara?"

I smiled at her. "Not quite..."

ROME

As I walked down the halls of the Vatican, I stopped just short of the fallen Cardinal after he was bodily hurled from the office door.

I didn't know that Vatican red tape could be so harsh.

A large African man in brilliant white stood in the door frame, his clenching fists ready to do more harm upon the Cardinal. "For the last time, Cupich, you will stop distorting Church doctrine, or you will find yourself in Singapore waiting to be defrocked. And if you think that *they* will tolerate your pagan practices any better than I do, please remember that they will jail you for spitting on the sidewalk and cane you bloody for minor vandalism. Now get out while I'm still of a mind to let you walk away. I will let you know if you are even still a Cardinal by the end of the week. If you're lucky, I will send you to Beijing so you can be one of their state-sanctioned church cronies."

The Cardinal scrambled to his feet and was about to protest when he bumped into me. He took one look at my rough and rumpled appearance and flinched away, as though worried I was contagious.

He looked back into the doorway and said, "You can't do this to me!"

I coughed. "Actually, he can. He's the Pope."

The Cardinal left. Pope Pius XIII, formerly Joshua Kutjok of

Uganda, waved me in. "Come in, Detective Nolan. I would like to chat with you about all of your good works and good deeds."

I walked for the Pope's office, and he said under his breath, "It is the first time I've met a saint."

I sighed as I took a seat. "Saints are dead, Your Holiness."

"Yes, I know. But at current rate of speed, that may become an issue sooner rather than later."

I rolled my eyes. "That's one way to put it."

The Pope leaned back in his chair, the desk chair designed for his bulk. "Also, call me Josh."

I shrugged. "Sure."

The Pope folded his hands across his immense chest. "So, you met one of my predecessors."

I nodded. "JP Two. Yes."

"In your report, you say that Pope Saint John Paul II told you that, '*You protect your family. You protect strangers. You bring them into your house, into your life. You have adopted many simply because they had nowhere else to go.*' Is there a particular reason you remembered that statement word for word?"

I nodded. "I took the hint."

The Pope cocked his head. "As a sign to do what?"

"To adopt the little girl, Lena, and bring her home. She was all for the idea. So was Mariel. Would you like to meet her?"

The Pope smiled. "Of course, when you have the time."

I thought about it for a moment, making sure the message got through. "She'll be here in a minute."

The Pope raised a brow. "Really? Are you certain that it's safe to leave her alone?"

One of the many things Pope Pius XIII did upon being elected was to personally crack down on the support system for the child molesters within the church. The "sexual liberation" of the sixties and seventies, combined with a large collection of people who wanted nothing more than to screw up the church's relationship with the laity, led to the creation of "lavender semi-naries," started by what would turn into our very own clerical gay mafia.

When elected, Pope Pius XIII did a world tour, meeting and shaking hands with many public figures within the church. The thing was, after the first four men got a handshake, the fourth was laid out, in public, by the pontiff, who had the local police waiting in the wings. It had been decades, if not centuries, since the staff of the Papal Office had been used as a weapon. Pius XIII had made certain that his staff was made from a good, sturdy iron. The better for cracking heads.

I shrugged. "I'm sure Lena's safe. Other people is a different question."

The Pope smiled. "Good."

"However, Father Pearson is with her. So I don't expect anything to happen."

"Ah. That makes more sense. What does your son think about this?"

"I called and asked him if he wanted an older sister. He said no, but he'd take a new friend."

The Pope smiled gently. "How cute." He looked over my loose fitting sweatsuit. "Tell me about the Golems?"

"What in particular would you like to know?"

"The golem clay formed around you. Which means that the pieces and parts of the golems never truly die. According to the legends, they are, at most, deactivated. If they could form armor around your body, why could they not reform?"

I grinned. "Who says they didn't? I returned as many to Rabbi Weil as would go. I figured he could use them. Europe needs to be fixed."

The Pope blinked, taken aback. I didn't blame him. The thought of dozens of golems let loose through Europe was a little scary. The original purpose of the golem was to protect Jewish populations. With all of Europe under threat from any of a half dozen different problems, it was one of the few ways to fight back.

"Who will control them?" the Pope asked.

"Various and sundry Rabbis in high-risk areas," I answered. "No more than one per city. Some were only one per region. Some of the smaller nations took one for the whole country." I gave a polite little cough and added, "Also, perhaps a few went to Israel. I didn't ask too many questions at that point."

The Pope nodded slowly and looked me right in the eye. "How many Golems wouldn't go with the Rabbis?"

Ah, he caught that. I shrugged. "Maybe three or four."

"How can you tell?"

"It's a rough estimate," I hedged, trying not to answer.

The Pope nodded slowly. "I do hope that you are ready for what comes next. Father Pearson reported the exorcism of Asmodeus. If the demon is to be believed, something wicked this way comes."

I smiled. With a thought, the clay that had gathered at my shirt slid out across my body, covering my clothes, the limbs, and even my face. Emblazoned on the front was the Crusaders' cross. My helmet was classic First Crusade plate mail. My fists were covered by gauntlets. The diamond of the Soul Ring was the only exposed part of me. It glowed and twinkled as it absorbed the prayers and charity of the Vatican and the surrounding monasteries, convents, and churches. The face mask cut off my vision, but it was replaced with a full Heads Up Display that revealed things that my sight could never pick up without augmentation.

"Let it come."

AN EXCERPT FROM DEUS VULT

Saint Tommy's adventure comes to a close in Deus Vult, Book Six! Read the first chapter of it now!

DEUS VULT

St. Tommy, NYPD Book Six

Chapter 1: Visitation

My name is Detective Tommy Nolan and I am a Saint.

More importantly, I am father to two beautiful daughters, and a son that was becoming more colorful by the day.

I held one of them in my arms. My two-month old daughter, Grace Gabrielle Nolan, squirmed and laughed in my embrace, nuzzling me, trying to bury herself deeper in my body.

I just sat back on the front porch swing and held her close. I was strangely content.

Perhaps it wasn't that strange. The front porch was to a New England summer house owned by

our local Medical Examiner, Doctor Sinead Holland. It had a few acres of land, and the edge of the property line wasn't a fence, but a treeline. While it wasn't summer, it was still an early spring. The air was crisp, but pleasant.

"She's a cuddler," my wife, Mariel, stated as she sat next to me. Mariel had long, wavy chestnut brown hair, round, deep-brown eyes, a pleasant heart-shaped face, and a healthy olive complexion. She wore a red and white floral cotton midi dress that set off her figure very nicely. Her Espadrille wedges were her pride and joy, giving height without sacrificing comfort. But she could wear a burlap sack and I'd still want to keep making babies with her.

She also looked out at the kids playing in the yard. Though "playing" was a strange word for it.

My son Jeremy threw things up into the air while our newly-adopted daughter, Lena, proceeded to hit them with objects that she tossed with her mind.

Yes. Lena tossed them with her mind. A telekinetic teenager wasn't the strangest thing that I had ever come across in my life—or even the last two years—and it was less supernatural, and more science fiction. Only without the fiction. A friendly neighborhood theologian (yes, there are such

beings] says such things are called preternatural, not supernatural.

"Pull!" Lena called, her thick Polish accent making it sound like pool.

Jeremy threw a fistful of grapes into the air. A box of toothpicks to Lena's right sprang to life as a collection of them darted out like shotgun flechette, each grape speared by a single toothpick.

Then, as much as to show off as to not waste food, Lena plucked each grape out of the air (with her mind) and piled them on a plate on her left.

Mariel laughed at the display. "She's fitting in well."

I smiled at her, then at Grace. "It helps that we have a flexible definition of 'normal.' " I leaned down to touch the tip of my nose to Grace's. "Don't we, Gracie?" I asked her.

Grace giggled. I touched my forehead to hers. "Headbutt of love."

Mariel wrapped an arm around me and leaned into me.

It was idyllic.

The front door opened and my partner, Alex Packard, stepped out onto the front porch. He wore khakis and a matching polo shirt. He covered a yawn as he looked out at the children playing. He ran his hand over what little hair he had left. "Well, Tommy, I have to hand it to you. You know how to collect colorful characters."

I ignored my partner. Sardonic, sarcastic, and cynical were his default positions.

Mariel lightly nudged him with her foot. "Oh, leave off, Alex. You like her, too."

Alex shrugged casually. "Sure. She's a nice kid. And she hasn't made my brain explode. Which is even better."

Mariel sighed, dismissing Alex's comment. I said nothing as I focused on the bundle of joy in my arms. Grace was such a strangely perfect little baby. I didn't remember Jeremy being anything like that when he was born. He had been eager to get out of the womb, and came out swinging, his little fists eager to latch on or touch something—usually as fast as possible.

Besides, if I replied to Alex's comment, I might have to mention that when I had first found Lena, it had been only a few feet from what was left of the men who kidnapped her. They had each been horribly murdered. Lena had done it with her mind. Though to say that they didn't have it coming would be a lie. But spreading that around would have probably only served to make people a little touchy around her. Just a guess on my part.

But in the two months since I had brought Lena home from Europe, she blended in like we had raised her from birth.

Jeremy and Lena ran up to the house. Jeremy wore a black sweatsuit. Lena wore a frilly pink dress that we could barely get her out of ever since we bought it—she'd seen it in the store, fell in love with it immediately, and would have slept in it if we didn't suggest that it might be ruined. She beamed as she ran after my son, showing how pretty she really was.

Jeremy ran up with the plate held up in front of him. "Look what Lena did!" he boasted on her behalf.

I nodded. "I saw. Very nicely done. Really good aim."

Lena beamed. She even bounced a little.

Alex smiled sardonically. "Hey, Jeremy, I thought you didn't like girls."

Jeremy looked at Alex like he took offense. "Lena's not a girl," he said in her defense. "She's awesome."

I smiled at them both. "Come on guys, let's go inside. I'm cooking omelets."

The children cheered. Alex smiled sleepily. Mariel kissed me on the cheek before she got up to join them.

Jeremy stopped, pivoted to face me, and asked, "Daddy, what's Mary like?"

I stopped halfway to standing up. I frowned and furrowed my brow. "Um ... personally? Why do you think I would know?"

"Well, who visited you before you got your superpowers?"

I paused, confused, cuddling Grace close to me. "I met John Paul II last month. Does that count?"

Jeremy frowned, confused. "In stories I've read, someone shows up before you get the charisms. So who talked to you?"

"Sorry ... no one did."

Jeremy blinked. "Huh." He shrugged, and we went inside.

Doctor Sinead Holland was already up and setting the kitchen table. I guess I'm predictable, I thought. I had spent the last few days getting up, walking to church for 6 a.m. mass, and coming home to find the house alive, awake, and ready for food.

Sinead smiled at me. She was a pretty brunette with a smile on her lips, and brown eyes that always caught the light. Her background was Northern European, up near Norway, giving her high cheekbones, and eyes that were nearly Asiatic. She wore a green and red madras cotton shirt (a few years old) and some loose faded jeans, plus a straw sunhat with wide green band. Her shoes were Israeli army issue, which are sturdy enough for farm work and go with any outfit. She managed to look polished despite "dressing country." Her words, not mine.

"Good walk this morning, Tommy?" she asked knowingly.

"It was good," I said, as always. I hadn't actually told anyone that I spent my mornings at church. Everyone figured it out already, but everyone had allowed me to not discuss it.

It wasn't that I was embarrassed to go to church, but I didn't want to talk about my visits to church. My relationship with God had become both simple and complex at the same time. He had granted me charisms in abundance—powers and abilities that came directly from God, and only manifested by Saints. I had a box in the trunk of my car that was directly powered by God. The ring on my finger was a mystic rock that had real-world effects to heal humans and hurt demons—it might as well have been the Ark of the Covenant.

Everyone else thought it was obvious that I would be a canonized a saint. While I've stopped trying to talk them out of it, I didn't have another explanation. While I wasn't complaining that my son thought I was a superhero, or that I had been able to defeat the forces of darkness multiple times via the grace of God Himself, my constant question was, Why me?

The only answer I kept getting was, Why not?

As I cooked breakfast on the stove top, operating four fry pans at a time, Alex entertained the kids with yet another magic trick. He kept giving me vague hints that it had saved his life at least once while I was away, but we hadn't gotten around to discussing that yet.

Alex held up an ace of spades. "This one really isn't a magic trick. This is an ordinary playing card. Nothing special about it.

Touch it, feel it, don't bend it out of shape, though. The edges aren't modified in any way, shape or form."

Once Lena and Jeremy were done examining the card, they offered it to Sinead. The good doctor smiled, raised her hands, and shook her head. "Thanks, but I've seen this trick."

Jeremy shrugged and handed it back to Alex. Jeremy leaned back against Lena, and she leaned into him.

Alex placed a grapefruit at the center of the table, and leaned back in his chair to create a little

more distance. He lined up the grapefruit with the card, and snapped his wrist forward. The card sliced into the grapefruit, driving half of the card into the fruit.

Alex brought the chair down with a thump. "It's literally all in the wrist!"

Lena laughed and clapped. "I want to do it!"

Lena looked at the pack of playing cards on the table. The top card shot off the deck and sliced into the grapefruit at one end and halfway out the other.

Ten other cards shot out one after another, turning the grapefruit into a pincushion of playing cards.

Alex looked from the grapefruit to Lena. "Show-off."

Lena merely smiled at him. She and Jeremy shared a high five.

I said nothing and kept cooking.

Then the doorbell rang.

I turned the heat down low on all the burners with my left hand, and grabbed my gun with my right. Alex was already out of the chair and grabbing his gun. It was before nine in the morning, so it wasn't the mail. And this was a summer home. It was rare for anyone to be here. If we were lucky, it was someone looking for an empty house to rob or squat in. If not...

Alex looked at Sinead. "Does anyone know you're at home?"

She shook her head. "Only my husband, and he's not due in for a few days."

Alex and I moved to the door. He braced himself to the side, and I had my hand on the handle. I was torn between checking the peephole and just opening the door so we could get the drop on whoever was on the other side.

This wasn't paranoia. This was Tuesday.

"Detective Nolan," came a British accent through the door. "I would appreciate it if you didn't shoot me."

The stress left my body, but entered my soul. It was one part of my world I hoped would never again come near my daily life and threaten my family.

I opened the door, and there stood Father Michael Pearson. He was a terribly average-looking priest. He was of medium height, with a sturdy build. The build was deceptive, since I had seen him in hand-to-hand combat. Pearson wore typical black-on-black-on-black for his pants, shirt and jacket. He was bald, mid-forties, with a closely-cropped brown beard. His eyes were brown and warm and friendly, hidden behind glasses with black frames so thick they looked like they had been borrowed from Clark Kent.

Except Pearson was my partner when I worked missions for the Vatican. I only saw him when something world-destroying needed to be stopped, or when the fate of millions hung over a pit.

Pearson smiled at me. "Detective Nolan, you're needed."

DEUS VULT is COMING SOON from Silver Empire. Join our mailing list to get notified when it is available!

REVIEW REQUEST

Did you enjoy the book?

Why not tell others about it? The best way to help an author and to spread word about books you love is to leave a review.

If you enjoyed reading CRUSADER, can you please leave a review on Amazon for it? Good, bad, or mediocre, we want to hear from *you*. Declan and all of us at Silver Empire would greatly appreciate it.

Thank you!

ACKNOWLEDGMENTS

I'd like to start by thanking all of the usual suspects.

Gail and Margaret Konecsni of Just Write! Ink, Hans Schantz, Jim McCoy, Daniel Humphreys, Russell and Morgon Newquist, and L. Jagi Lamplighter—for all of the edits, suggestions, reviews and encouragement.

Thanks to all of the Kickstarter backers who made these awesome covers possible.

Thanks to Larry Correia's Monster Hunter International Facebook group for the gun data.

And, as always, Vanessa.

I'd like to note that the references used over the course of this book include *The Rite* by Matt Baglio and *An Exorcist Tells His Story* by Father Amorth. This includes the rise of Occultism in Europe and the tales of a Catholic priest who specializes in the occult and who works with the SAS. In real life, his name is Father Aldo Buonaiuto.

There are several places in Germany and in Poland that I took many, many liberties with. However, the ruins of East Germany are real, and are they a wreck. Here, the ruins of the Blankenburg barracks referred to at "Morderberg" is set in what was East

Berlin. From what I can tell, it has been torn down relatively recently—though it should have been concreted over and the ground sown with salt. But what was there is described to the best of my ability. I took liberties with the building design, but not the layout. As for the description of Morderberg as a cross between The Great Grimpen Mire and Mordor, I may have made it sound too appealing.

Declan Finn lives in a part of New York City unreachable by bus or subway. Who's Who has no record of him, his family, or his education. He has been trained in hand to hand combat and weapons at the most elite schools in Long Island, and figured out nine ways to kill with a pen when he was only fifteen. He escaped a free man from Fordham University's PhD program, and has been on the run ever since. There was a brief incident where he was branded a terrorist, but only a court order can unseal those records, and really, why would you want to know?

BB bookbub.com/authors/declan-finn

f facebook.com/DeclanFinnBooks

twitter.com/DeclanFinnBooks

SILVER EMPIRE

Keep up with all the new releases, sneak peeks, appearances and more with the empire. Sign up for our Newsletter today!

Or join fellow readers in our Facebook Fan Group, the Silver Empire Legionnaires. Enjoy memes, fan discussions and more.

CRUSADER

ST. TOMMY, NYPD BOOK FIVE

By Declan Finn

Published by Silver Empire

https://silverempire.org/

This is a work of fiction. Names, characters, businesses, places, events and incidents are either the products of the author's imagination or used in a fictitious manner. Any resemblance to actual persons, living or dead, or actual events is purely coincidental.

Cover by Steve Beaulieu